Dead Calendar

By:

Ken Kirkberry

Copyright © Ken Kirkberry 2019

This book is sold subject to the condition that it shall not, by way of trade or otherwise, be lent, resold, hired out, or otherwise circulated without the publisher's prior consent in any form of binding or cover other than that in which it is published and without a similar condition including this condition being imposed on the subsequent publisher.

The moral right of Ken Kirkberry has been asserted. ISBN-13: 9781699636497

This is a work of fiction. Names, characters, businesses, organizations, places, events and incidents either are the product of the author's imagination or are used fictitiously. Any resemblance to actual persons, living or dead, events, or locales is entirely coincidental.

Ken Kirkberry is a lifelong daydreamer who has finally placed his thoughts into print.

Ken has been brought up on Sci-Fi in both print and film format. Through the Enlightenment trilogy of books these views are explored. However, with a second love of crime and fantasy Ken has, with this book provided his second fast paced, gripping genre of - Crime.

CONTENTS

Monday, Dec 1st	1
Tuesday, Dec 2nd	5
Wednesday, Dec 3rd	13
Thursday, Dec 4th	19
Friday, Dec 5th	28
Saturday, Dec 6th	39
Sunday, Dec 7th	51
Monday, Dec 8th	60
Tuesday, Dec 9th	67
Wednesday, Dec 10th	78
Thursday, Dec 11th	88
Friday, Dec 12th	92
Saturday, Dec 13th	95
Sunday, Dec 14th	99
Monday, Dec 15th	111
Tuesday, Dec 16th	121
Wednesday, Dec 17th	127
Thursday, Dec 18th	131
Friday, Dec 19th	146
Saturday, Dec 20th	155
Monday, Dec 22nd	157

Monday, December 1

Carl Hughes walked through the final security door, retina detection allowing access to the small but high-tech room. Five desks, each with a large central monitor in front of the seat and seven smaller screens around the main one. Carl walked to his seat, just before sitting he acknowledged the two female colleagues at the desks to the right of his. "Hi Ladies," he gave a small wave as he spoke.

The first seated woman, who was slightly older than the other women, turned in her seat. Denise said, "Hi, Carl. We will finish in a minute and then it is all yours."

Smiling as he sat Carl heard a giggle. Turning his head, he caught the younger woman, Charlotte, who was sitting at the desk furthest from his, go red and look the other way. Carl ignored the movement and pushed the keyboard enter button; the GCHQ emblem came up in the middle of the screen requesting logging-in details. Carl entered his password then looked at the facial recognition camera. His screens lit up, showing varied information data and sources.

Charlotte got up and left. Denise stood to follow but stopped and turned back addressing Carl, "I'm sorry Carl, but asking Charlotte out on a date last week was not the best idea."

Carl went red in the face; "I know…I thought…never mind. Overweight and nerd glasses!"

Denise took a closer step towards her colleague and put a hand on his shoulder. "Hey, look the right girl will come along someday. Charlotte is what…barely twenty-one?"

Carl looked up at his colleague. "I'm thirty-eight and have never married, when is someday?"

Denise smiled, "If I was not married?"

Carl giggled, "Thanks, Denise, but I know you never mean it when you say that."

Denise giggled, "I'll get you a coffee before I go."

Coffee delivered, Carl sat watching the main screen eyes darting to the smaller screens as text popped up or cameras showed changes. Two hours passed and Carl had managed to bring up a chess game to pass the time. His security surveillance of world communications was essential, but with modern technology, the systems did most of the work for him.

Carl ignored the two-thousandth terrorist word pick up from monitored sources, having to hit acknowledge every time to clear the message. Looking to move his Queen he sat back as his main screen crackled and came up with a Santa Clause figure in the middle with a message:

Ho, Ho, Ho,

Merry Xmas to you all!

The image and message disappeared in a second. Carl went to hit the 'All Monitors' button, but one of his other colleagues had got there first. Alert messages sprung up at the bottom of all the screens. Carl started typing in the security code that would block any virus attacks at the same time as recording and seeking where the last five minutes' messages had come from. His desk phone rang and he picked up the handset, "Carl. What have you got?"

"Nothing yet Boss, but I think it is benign!"

Major Martin, Carl's superior, added, "Okay. Stay on it, and I will be with you in ten minutes."

Within ten minutes, Major Martin was standing next to Carl. Other colleagues joined Martin. "What do you think, Carl?"

"It has gone…even the recording. I have no trace. Has anyone else got it?"

Martin replied, "No. Ten of you on the monitors and none of you got it. You said it is benign, so we are safe?"

"Yes, Sir. No apparent traces or anything left."

"Okay, you lead. Triple check then get us back running. I will call the Defence Secretary and advise him. Any more tonight and we shut down."

Tuesday, December 2

Sharon Mansell shouted, "Alexa snooze!" before turning over trying to get back to sleep.

Her husband, Ken, was lying in bed next to her. He is the same age as his wife, although dark-haired to her blonde. He was as physically in shape as her as both had a love of exercise. Ken kicked his leg into Sharon's back, "Get up. It is your turn for tea. I'm hitting the shower."

Sharon fell out of the bed, whispered something under her breath and left the bedroom heading for the kitchen to make a couple of teas. Little was said between the couple as the daily routine took shape, each using the toilet facilities, showing and dressing alternatively. Tea finished, Ken put on his shoes. "I'm being picked up. I have a meeting out of town. You?"

Sharon took the last swig of her tea, "I'm at the House, some security meeting. I'll take the scooter."

Ken kissed his wife and headed out of their London flat. Sharon left ten minutes later, taking the electric scooter the short one-mile ride to the Houses of Parliament. "Morning, Mrs Mansell!" the police guard at the Houses of Parliament's gate shouted as she arrived.

"Hi, Nick. Do you want to frisk me?" Sharon said with a giggle.

Nick looked at the shapely woman, *his age* he thought—*mid-thirties—fit.* "Sorry, Mrs Mansell but your husband is more senior than us both, so I will have to give it a miss. I need my job."

Sharon laughed as she opened her coat, revealing the holstered weapon above her blouse. Sharon Mansell was one of the new World Communication and Security Team (WCST) and one of the few people allowed into the Houses of Parliament armed.

A short while later and Sharon had joined a meeting. As she looked out of the window over the Thames, taking in the old MI5 building on the opposite side. She felt a nudge to her side. "Look interested, Sharon!" Dean Hamilton her superior whispered as he sat next to her.

"One and a half hours already. Sorry, Boss." Dean had been Sharon's superior for nearly five years. He too was a military veteran and older by a decade.

Although suited, he kept trim for his age and was happy to support the new chiselled beard trend.

---*---

In an office building in Geneva, Helmut Bopp looked out of his office window. From this view, he could see the Palace of Nations, the home of the United Nations opposite. Bopp opened the window slightly and listened while he checked his watch. *On-time* he thought as he could hear the drums. Closing the window, Bopp turned to put on his coat and exited the office.

"The Secret Drum Corp, Mr Bopp?"

Bopp smiled at his secretary, "Yes. I will take lunch now and listen to them."

His secretary stood, removed a flask of soup that she had previously heated and gave it to her boss. "It is a little cold today, but tradition must not be broken," Smiling, she handed over the flask.

Bopp smiled, "Yes. Although my wife does not play for them anymore, listening to them reminds me of how we met." With this, he left the building and took up position next to a lamppost on the kerb and awaited the band parade to come past him. The tradition was popular and more locals were present than tourists, all were standing on one curb. The railings on the other side, by the Palace, were for Police and Security Forces only.

Bopp noticed a lady with a young child behind him. Smiling, he moved a little closer to the lamppost signalling the lady and child to get to the kerb. "Thank you, Sir. And a Merry Christmas!" the child called to Bopp. Bopp smiled and turned to take in the band some ten metres from him. He was humming to the music in his head.

Behind the woman next to Bopp, a fat man stood, his brow was full of sweat even though it was cold. As the band came alongside Bopp, the fat man shouted. The fat man then pushed the woman and child aside and stood just in front of Bopp. The front drummer stopped adjacent to the fat man and looked at him. Bopp went to pull the man back, but his heart sank. The man pulled his coat open to show a terrorist bomb waistcoat, and with one hand, he pulled the detonator. The explosion was loud and the blast blew out windows, bins, street furniture and people within twenty metres.

---*---

Sharon looked at her silent but vibrating mobile. Taking in the message she immediately whispered to her boss, Dean. "Boss. A suicide bomb in Geneva. I need to go."

Dean did not reply. Sharon stood, smiled at the meeting chairman, and left the room. Outside in a corridor, she was able to read the message in full. Heading to the secure communications room within the House she asked immediately on entry, "Smith, what is the news from Geneva?"

Agent Smith did not respond but pointed to the BBC news on the screen. Sharon took in the story:

A suicide bomber has struck in Geneva outside the United Nations building. Twenty-three believed dead: men, women, and children, including members of the famous Secret Drum corps...

Sharon sat on a desk and her heart sank. *Bastard*, she thought. "What is the real news, Smith?"

"Nothing in detail yet. It is too soon."

"I'll call Sara," Sara Lietman, her WCST colleague in Switzerland, was not answering and obviously busy.

It took three-quarters of an hour before Sara returned the call.

"Hi, Sharon. It is awful, twenty-six dead including eight children who were listening to Christmas songs!"

Sharon could hear the tears in her friend's voice as she spoke. "I am so sorry, Sara. Is there anything formal? Has anyone claimed responsibility?"

"No, not yet. But we have eyewitness reports suggesting a middle eastern-looking man might have been the bomber."

Sharon thought, "Switzerland. No?"

Sara wiped some tears and hesitated a bit. "The UN building was right opposite but some distance from the bomb. It is not affected."

"Then, the victims?"

"Too early, my friend. Look, I have to go, but I will update you as soon as we have more." With this, Sara hung up.

Sharon spent the remainder of the afternoon trying to capture as much information as possible using the House's communication rooms' facilities to the full. "Hi, dear!" Sharon spoke into her mobile.

"Hi Honey. You have been busy. I guess you are dealing with the Geneva bomb?"

"Yes. It is awful. Children dead!"

"Look, I am with the Home Secretary and we are heading for the House. A COBRA meeting. Will you be there around six when we get there?"

"Yes, I will. Catch you then, honey. Love you."

Sharon saw her husband as he arrived, but they did not have a chance to talk as he headed straight to the Prime Minister's office then off to the COBRA meeting. Sharon had attended these meetings on occasion, but Ken was the Home Secretary's permanent civil service advisor. It was just after eight when Ken walked into the House bar, seeing his wife he headed straight to her. Pausing first to kiss her he soon asked, "So what is the news?"

After both Mansell's sat down Sharon spoke, "We do not think it is a bomb against the UN. As yet none of the victims who are known are involved with the UN, although not all are identified yet."

Ken held his wife's hand for a moment and then let go to take the whiskey provided by a waiter. "Thank you. Dean said similar in the COBRA meeting. I am sure he will fill you in. Did Sara provide any more information?"

"No. Sara did speak to me, but until they have all the names, she will not know."

"The bomber? Dean has no idea but possibly a middle-eastern terrorist?"

"Seems like it. Look I'm shattered, can we go home?"

Wednesday, December 3

Ken turned off the TV, having dressed quicker and earlier than usual he had decided to take in the morning news.

"What are they saying?"

Ken looked up at his wife, "Same as yesterday but blaming or at least implicating a variety of terrorist groups."

Sharon thought, "They know nothing. No messages so far on my side to add anything else. Will your driver drop me at the office as I assume you will be at Downing Street?"

"Yeah, sure. Let's go."

Sharon's first meeting was a debrief with Dean in their new offices by the Thames—a ten-minute walk from the Houses of Parliament. Sharon had received an update from Sara and various agencies that were interested in the case.

Dean called to Sharon, "Tea?"

"Sure. My head is spinning with this stuff."

Sat at the table in the small café in the office, Dean asked, "So what have you got?"

"Nothing of any substance or anything that holds a pattern apart from the obvious suicide bomb theory."

"The victims?"

"Again, no UN or government staff amongst them. Most office workers, a couple of bankers…that's it."

"The band?"

Sharon flicked her tablet screen. "Regardless of the name and the uniform they wear, they are not military. Two killed including the band leader, but again nothing stands out."

"The UN?"

"No, too far from the explosion. No windows were blown out or anything."

"Strange, a high-profile target area but not a high-profile target?"

Sharon stood, "Not yet. I'll get back on it."

Carl was watching the news at his desk, and Geneva was the focus. Major Martin entered the room. "Good evening, Carl. Terrible thing."

"Yes, Boss. Terrible."

"I have signed off your report about the Santa blip as a one-off for now, but it needs to be monitored."

"Sorry, Boss. I really cannot see where it came from or what it has done, but it seems to have gone. It's worrying, though!"

"Okay. We have followed protocol and made the Home Office aware and made COBRA aware but haven't received a response. This Geneva thing seems to have taken everyone's time. Anyway…" Martin stopped as Carl interrupted.

"Fuck! It did it again! Look!"

Martin looked at the screen just catching the Santa image disappearing. "What was it? Was it the same? What did it say?"

Carl frantically hit the keys on the keyboard. "Shut up! Sorry, Boss…leave me to get it!"

Carl continued pressing keys, his screen alive with code. Dean pushed the alert button, knowing his whole team would follow suit and lock down the system but still be able to trace the attack or any code or virus left behind.

Carl's brow began to sweat; he was speaking to himself as he pushed buttons…then he erupted. "Fuck! Fuck! Fuck!" Slamming his headphones on the desk, he stood and walked to the wall and hit it with the bottom of his fist.

"Calm down, Carl!" Martin ordered.

Turning around he took a deep breath. "Sorry, Boss. I lost it again, but it was there."

"What did it say?"

"I think, 'Ho, Ho, Ho,' but it had the number two at the end I think?"

Martin thought, "Are you sure. Did you capture it?"

"No. This guy is good. Well, whoever it is they are bloody good!"

"You calm down, and I will check with the others and report it."

---*---

Andy Borist looked at the message on his mobile's screen after hearing it beep. "Ken, what do you think of this?"

Ken was sitting in the back of the Jaguar next to the Home Secretary. Taking the mobile he read the message, "GCHQ has a blip. That is serious. I will call them, Sir."

"It is 9pm, Ken, leave it until the morning. It is not coded red."

"Are you sure, Sir?"

"Yes. Buttles will drop me first and you after as usual. But be early tomorrow." This was said with good timing as Buttles, the driver, pulled up outside the Home Secretary's house. Sergeant Roberts, Borist's bodyguard, exited the car first from the front passenger seat. He took in the surroundings, noting the Police outriders on either side, he let the Home

Secretary exit the car and go to the house. The car took off, Ken was home within fifteen minutes.

Noting Sharon already in bed reading Ken washed, changed and laid next to her. "Hard day?"

Sharon put her book down and snuggled up to her husband. "Yeah. We have nothing. Have you heard anything more?"

Ken thought, "No. Boris (Ken's nickname for his boss) seems to think it is local to the Swiss and has lowered the security level. I think he and the PM are more worried about the Police Commissioner's meeting next week and the budgets."

"Politicians!"

Ken chuckled. "Are you aware of the GCHQ breach?"

Sharon pulled a face, "No. When? What?"

"This evening some Santa prank thing jumped up on their screens."

"Wow, that's serious?"

"I thought so, but Boris did not seem worried. I will pick it up in the morning." With this, Ken kissed Sharon and turned over to sleep.

Thursday, December 4

Both the Mansell's attended different meetings. Ken managed to catch a mobile call around 3pm. "Hi Honey. So, GCHQ was twice this month, not just last night!" Sharon informed.

"Yeah. One of our juniors took the first on Monday but did not highlight it. Is it to do with Geneva?"

Ken thought the pause was strange. "We are not sure, and GCHQ has asked not to share this yet."

"Why not?"

"They are embarrassed that they may have been hacked."

Ken thought, "Idiots. I'll give that Martins a call and find out more, and if he does not respond to me, I'll send you in." Ken giggled as he said this.

Sharon laughed, "I'm sure they will respond to the Home Secretary rather than just poor little WCST."

Ken laughed, "He can just fire them, but you can go shoot them!"

Sharon laughed again. "Look, I will be late so let's catch a nightcap when I'm home."

"Love you, honey. Catch you later."

---*---

A little later in the day a military pipe band was taking to the stage in Edinburgh just below the castle. Although quite dark, the outside stage was well lit. Band conductor, Captain Mills, was ordering his team where to sit, and within minutes rehearsals started. Even though it was an hour before the start crowds were beginning to form in the park area in front of the stage for the free Christmas carol event.

Katrina Zelse entered the deserted office block with two men beside her. As they approached the reception desk, the security guard stood. "Good evening, Miss. What can I do for you?"

Zelse smiled, looked around, then removed a silenced gun from her belt. One shot and the security guard was dead. "Hide him. Tidy and lock up. I will see you upstairs!" she ordered the two men. Although the office building was being redecorated, the lifts were still working. Taking the lift to the twelfth floor, Zelse exited and walked to the office that overlooked the Castle. Looking out of the window she saw Edinburgh Castle less than three hundred metres away. Placing her larger bag on the floor, Zelse removed the glasscutter. Attaching the cutter to the window and turning the handle in a full circle the glass cut and the circle easily removed. Zelse felt the cold air come through the hole. Going back to her bag, she removed the rifle parts and assembled her weapon. Before attaching the sight, Zelse placed it in the newly made hole in the window and looked through. Zelse could just make out the sound from the band some hundred and fifty metres from her at the bottom of the castle. The band was on the stage and most were sitting, Zelse had time to set up her rifle before the show would start.

Captain Mills looked at his watch, 7pm. He turned to look at the crowd behind him, *a good turn out*, he thought. Turning back to face his band, he tapped the baton on the podium. The band stopped warming up and took their positions. Then there was silence.

Captain Mills raised his baton and with a whisk to his right, the Pipers piped up...the show had begun. Mills was in the swing of the show, two carols passed, and he could hear the crowd singing and enjoying themselves behind him. Pointing to the lead piper who stood to begin and smiled at him Mills went to smile back but shrieked in horror as he saw the piper's head explode. Time seemed to stand still. Then Mills dropped to the floor. The crowd screamed and started to run. The band all rose, but two more of their number hit the stage dead. A policeman came to his senses and looked up. He saw the sparks coming from the building opposite. With each spark someone dropped to the floor. Shouting into his radio, he called for help, "Sniper in the Old Caledonian Ash building. Quick we need armed support."

Zelse smiled as she aimed and fired. *Wow, I'm good,* with each pull of the trigger she saw someone fall. Her scope caught a policeman appearing to look up at her from a distance. Another trigger pull and he fell to the floor. By now the challenge got harder as the band and spectators had run or took cover. *Ahh*, she thought as she heard police sirens below her. Five shots saw to the first police car that had got to close to her building. Two further shots took out two police officers running toward her building.

Her concentration was disturbed as one of her colleagues called her. "Zelse let's move, you have killed enough!"

Zelse looked back at her colleague, ignored him and took to firing out the window again; three more random dots hit the floor. She jumped as her colleague pulled at her. "Get your hands off me, or you die!"

"Zelse, you need to put your rifle away. We are done, the place will be full of armed police shortly. We need to go!"

Zelse huffed but packed up her rifle and followed her men out. This time, ignoring the lift, they took to the stairs and headed up towards the roof. Zelse could hear the noise of more sirens below and caught a light in the sky heading their way. *A police helicopter no doubt,* she thought.

Upon reaching the roof, she and her men pulled out straps from their waists and attached them to a steel rope above. One of her colleagues jumped off the building's roof zip wiring to the smaller building next door. The second man followed, then Zelse. Once all three were on the opposite roof, one of the men disconnected the wire and threw it back towards the building they had just come from. Zelse smiled as she knew the police would not be checking this building for now and they could escape, undetected.

---*---

"Fuck no!" Sharon shouted through her mobile.

"Honey calm down!" Ken was trying to calm his wife.

"Sorry but an assassin in Edinburgh? No way. The Boss and I are going there now we have a helicopter picking us up. I won't be home tonight, honey!"

"Sharon go, just go, but please be careful. Honey, I love you!"

---*---

Sharon was right, they were in Edinburgh by 11pm. The police car they were in skidded to a halt just near the stage where the band had played earlier; Sharon and Dean jumped out of the vehicle. "Who is in charge here?" Dean asked as he held up his identity card.

Without answer a policeman pointed to another officer. Dean walked to the officer, Sharon in tow. "I am Senior Agent Hamilton, WCST!"

The uniformed Commissioner turned. "Dean, how are you?" Commissioner Fowler said.

Dean smiled; he knew Fowler. "Hi, Amos. What is the situation?"

"Fifteen dead at least. No trace of the shooter. Shots fired from the building over there, can you see the lights?" Dean followed the pointing finger and could see the office block opposite and what appeared like many flashing lights. These were police torches; the building was still being searched.

"Agent Mansell," Sharon introduced herself. "Is that where the sniper was?"

"Yes. What the fuck is going on, a sniper attack in Edinburgh!" Fowler was still in disbelief.

"Mansell, check the office block. I will stay with the commissioner!"

Sharon turned, grabbed the police officer who had brought them and ordered him to lead her to the office block. Within minutes Sharon was standing at the window where the sniper had been earlier. With forensics already on the scene, Sharon spoke to the senior officer, "Anything?"

"Not yet. Well, no obvious fingerprints on anything that we can tell. Most of the electrics in the building are off. Thankfully not the lifts."

"They got off the building on a zip wire?"

"Looks so." Calling to a colleague the senior officer ordered, "Take the agent to the roof and show her."

Sharon followed the Policeman to the roof; again, more forensics was present. Sharon was led to a steel rope circled on the roof floor. "WCST. What is going on here?"

A forensics officer replied, "We pulled this wire up as it was dangling from the roof. Our colleagues found an attachment on that building next door. They must have zip wired off and escaped from the rear of that building while our guys came to the front of this building."

Sharon spent another hour assessing the sniper building and then moved to the escape building. From the roof, she looked towards the square where the stage was. She could not make out the people but opened her mobile and called her boss. "Hi, Boss. Not much here but hopefully we will find fingerprints on some of the gear left."

Dean was still in the park, standing on the stage. He looked towards the office building knowing Sharon was at the top of one, but he could not make out any figures from where he was. "We have a room set up in the local police station. I will meet you there in a half-hour. The police driver will know where."

Friday, December 5

Sharon woke from her sleep, her back hurting. Looking around, she saw her boss in the chair opposite. He was still asleep and looked very uncomfortable. Rising to her feet, she saw a uniform policewoman standing at the door of the room she was in. "Morning, I assume? Toilets?"

"Good morning, Agent Mansell. Out the door second on the left. Can I get you some coffee?"

Sharon smiled, "Tea, white no sugar for me. The boss will have a strong black coffee. Thanks." Returning to the room, Sharon noted her boss was awake and already drinking the supplied coffee. "Morning, Boss. How's your back?"

Dean winced, "Buggered." Looking at the papers on the table before him he added, "Did we fall asleep while working?"

"Yes, you did!" Fowler said as he entered the room.

"Good morning, Commissioner," Sharon said taking a sip of her tea, "Only slept, what an hour or two, but enough to tell this was a professional job. No disrespect, but no one of note was amongst the dead, although the band is military."

"Not a lot, then!" Fowler shot Sharon down.

"Wow, Amos, easy!" Dean defended his agent.

Fowler took a sip of his coffee. "Sorry Dean. Now sixteen dead including five of my men!"

"I am sorry, Commissioner. We do think we know who the assassin is though."

Fowler looked at Sharon, "What, how?"

"Very few people could pull this off and the zip wire escape has been used before. I checked with my team last night and they found it used five years ago in Hong Kong when a senior politician was shot dead." Sharon paused for another sip of tea. "Anyhow our Chinese colleagues unusually gained some clues, and a Russian assassin called Zelse was responsible."

"So, we can find this guy?"

Sharon looked at Fowler. "Zelse is a woman. No, we, Interpol…basically everyone, have been looking for her for years."

"So how does this help?"

Dean decided to answer. "Look, Amos. Zelse is hard to get hold of, but if it is her, then we can look to see who is behind this. Zelse is a specialist and we have contacts that could lead us to her employer."

"I'll clean up a bit and will speak to the team. Commissioner." Sharon put her tea down and headed for the main operations room to speak with her police colleagues.

"She is one of the best, Amos. Let her look at this and make sure your team support her."

Fowler looked to Dean. "Yes, of course. She has my team's full support."

It was 2pm when the three met again for an update. Inspector Dracken, the police officer in charge of the case, spoke first. "Sixteen confirmed dead, ten wounded or injured. No one person stands out as an obvious target. No prints or other evidence to give away our murderer."

Fowler moved uncomfortably in his chair before replying. "So not royalty based as no shots were fired at the castle. Thankfully the royals were not here anyway. Mansell, you have a lead?"

Sharon looked to her boss. "We are confident we know the assassin is Katrina Zelse, and we have feelers out about her whereabouts and whoever paid her. This is already international as she is probably out of the UK already."

"Is this to do with the Geneva bomb?" Dracken asked.

Dean responded, "Not yet. Two different approaches, although both were bands playing Christmas songs. It would appear to have a religious focus and we are talking with our Swiss colleagues to see if they have found any direct link between these two atrocities."

---*---

In GCHQ, Denise was monitoring her screens. The Santa message had not been seen the previous day and was expected today. More surveillance software had been installed.

Denise jumped, although earlier than previously, the Santa message had blipped up again. Denise hit the alert button but also pushed in some code. "Yes!" she screamed to herself as she caught the picture.

Ho, Ho, Ho – 3!

Denise got straight on the phone to her boss. Martin was with her within minutes. "Denise, what have you got?" Martin called as he entered the room.

"I have the picture. Look!"

Martin studied the screen. "Wow, well done! Check the systems. I will tell everyone!"

---*---

Sharon sat thinking, *this meeting is not going anywhere*, she was happy to feel her mobile vibrating. Looking at the screen she read the message aloud then stood. All around her went quiet. "Boss. GCHQ has something of interest. May I leave the meeting?"

Dean looked at Fowler, then replied to Sharon. "Yes, go. Commissioner, I need to go as well." Dean and Sharon were in the hallway outside the meeting room.

Sharon finished her call. "GCHQ had another blip, but they have caught the screen dump."

Dean thought. "Our support team has arrived and I do not think anything else will happen here. So, we should visit GCHQ." Sharon did not need any further instruction and within the hour they were in a helicopter heading for GCHQ.

At 9pm Sharon was being introduced to Major Martin. She knew many of the staff, but Martin was new, having been transferred from another military unit. Pleasantries over Sharon and Dean were led to the small surveillance room. As Sharon entered the room, a smile came to her face as she greeted Carl, a welcome surprise. "Hi, Carl. Long-time no see." Carl was both a colleague and friend to Sharon.

Carl stood from his chair and greeted Sharon with a hug. Martin broke up the reunion all too soon, "Tell them, Carl."

Carl sat down with the three visitors standing over his shoulder as he pressed some keys, the captured Santa file image came up on his screen. "We have had three messages. All the same as this but with a different number on. Today's was 3."

"A count up to what? You cannot trace it?" Sharon asked.

"No. Nothing, the hacker is good, very good."

Dean asked, "Apart from the screen pop up there is no obvious virus or data capture?"

Carl looked uncomfortable, "No, Sir. Nothing."

Dean turned on Martin, "So why have we only been told now?"

Martin went on the defensive, "We followed procedure and the Home Office and COBRA were advised."

"But you decided to mark it as only a minor threat?"

Martin was uncomfortable, "I am following procedure. There is no obvious loss of data or control of systems. We've dealt with quite a few of these lately. Normally thirteen-year-old kids trying us out!"

Before Dean could answer Sharon interjected, "Hey, we are here to find out what is going on not to argue with each other. Major, have we spoken to other agencies?" Martin looked quizzical. Sharon continued, "Have we informed our foreign friends. Have they seen the same thing as say the Swiss?"

Dean picked up where this was going and spoke. "Martin. We need a meeting room to contact the other countries' surveillance co-ordinators. Especially the Swiss!"

Martin was still defensive, "Look we do not go around telling the world that GCHQ has been penetrated until we have to. I will speak to the Home Secretary and the Defence Secretary first!"

Dean smiled, "That was not a request. It was an order!"

Martin did not continue to argue but led Dean out, Sharon stayed to talk to her friend. "A bit of an arse don't you think, Carl?"

Carl smiled, "Yes, but he is new and sticking to the rule book. Funny, he did not know your husband is virtually the Home Secretary. How is Ken?"

Sharon smiled, "Good but working hard, as we all are. How are you doing, anyone special?"

Carl went red, "No. I am a geek. Once a geek always a geek."

Sharon put her arm around her seated friend, "Come on, you are a good guy. Maybe you work too hard and spend too much time here on the screens and probably at home?"

"Busted!" Carl replied.

Sharon laughed, "I will dance with you again this year if you invite me to the office Christmas party."

Carl looked at her fondly. She had indeed danced with him the last couple of parties and only a few months ago been out for a drink with him and some colleagues. Visiting GCHQ was part of her job. "I thought I had already sent you the invite."

Sharon giggled, "Must have lost the email!" She knew Carl would turn his eyes up at this. "So, back to the serious stuff, you are our best IT man, and you don't have anything to add?"

Carl thought, "No, sorry, Sharon. It is a blip with no trace."

Sharon looked at the image again. "Look get a copy to my team to look at. The Santa is not traditional looking. I would say American in style?"

Carl looked at the image, "Wow, how did you guess that?"

"Too many US Christmas films." Sharon giggled. "I'll catch up with the boss. Tea later?"

"Of course. I'll see you in the canteen in about an hour when I have my break."

As Sharon headed towards the meeting room and opening the door, she was nearly pushed over as Martin exited in a rush. Sharon looked at the leaving Martin and said out loud, "Well, excuse me!" There was no response. Sharon closed the door behind her and sat on a windowsill near her seated boss. "You pissed him off I see?"

"Sorry, but yes. Martin is a good man, but he has to look outside the rulebook sometimes. Although he is blaming your husband's office and the defence office for not picking up on his low-risk alarm." Dean chuckled to himself. "Anyway, the hack is not just the UK."

Sharon was taken aback, "The Swiss?"

"Yes. Exact the same since Monday. Even at the same time or at least in local time to ours. Plus, the Germans and the Italians and the Americans that we know of."

"Wow. This is serious if linked to the two recent atrocities. Let me make some calls and I will let you know."

"That's what I pay you for. I need to go and save a possibly suicidal major."

Saturday, December 6

10am and after a night of calls and messages Sharon's mobile rang. "Hi Honey, please say something good I hardly slept last night."

Ken giggled, "I bet you look like shit!"

"Bastard. That does not help!" Sharon also giggled. She continued by filling her husband in on what was found and the links to at least eight other confirmed countries' security services.

"And the Russians?" Ken asked.

"Not confirmed yet. They will be the last to be open and honest."

"Your friend Helga, she would know?"

Although alone in the room, Sharon looked around. "Yes, I spoke to her, and unofficially they do have it."

Ken shook his head, "And that is why we set up the WCST to share this kind of info. I will push Boris later and get him to find out more. Oh, we have nothing further on Zelse, but the world is looking."

"My team in London have been looking at the two incidents and trying out anything they can to see if there is a link. Nothing as yet. Wait did you say you were seeing Boris later?"

"Yeah. I am off to a COBRA meeting shortly, so we will stay there until the dinner in the House later. I may as well work; you are some miles away, dear."

Sharon laughed, "Look, I am hungry and I stink so will find somewhere to crash for a few hours and try and freshen up."

"I told you that you looked shit!" Ken laughed to himself as the phone was put down.

Sharon was able to catch a couple of hours sleep in one of the night staff rooms and a shower was a blessing. Carl had popped out to buy a change of top for her. Both were in a meeting room with Dean, Martin and the GCHQ senior officer, General Buck. Buck started the meeting, describing the situation to date as known. An hour in and the screens were filled with other faces, GCHQ, the Home Office, the Defence Office, MI5, and MI6 plus the Met Police as all were now involved. It was necessary, but the meeting dragged on; Sharon looked at her watch, and it was nearly 7pm.

---*---

Ken was behind the Home Secretary heading to the events hall inside the House of Lords. Even though they were in the house, Roberts was in front of the Home Secretary. Standard practice now that the threat level was at red. Roberts got irritated as Boris shook as many people's hands as he could as he entered the hall, picking up a glass of wine as he walked. "Sir!" was all Roberts said as he took his boss' arm by the elbow. Within a minute or two, the Home Secretary was sitting at the head of the table overlooking the room. Roberts sat just behind on a chair with Ken next to him. The Home Secretary stood and welcomed his guests then started his speech about the arts charity he was honouring.

Roberts pulled out his mobile and looked at the picture of his beautiful wife and two very young children. The text he feared came through from his brother, *I am in place, and God be with you!* A tear came to Roberts' eye; for a moment, he froze. Finally, he stood, pulled out his weapon, and blew the back of the Home Secretary's head off. Turning he aimed at the seated Minister of Arts and emptied two bullets into his head.

Ken responded and went to grapple Roberts. Roberts pushed him aside and raised his gun to Ken's head. Ken felt it took ages, but it was only a second or so as he looked at the barrel of a gun. Roberts said below his breath, "Sorry, please look after my family." With that, he pulled the trigger, and the bullet whizzed past Ken's head. Blood covered Ken's face as Roberts fell to the floor in front of him.

"Are you okay, Sir?" Ken came to his senses, one of the other security guards at his side, his weapon also to hand.

"I am okay. The Home Secretary?" Ken took in the scene. The Home Secretary's body was slumped over the table; the white tablecloth was red with his blood and that of the Arts Secretary. Roberts' body was in a pool of blood below him.

"Sir, let's get you out of here!" Ken did not reply. With this, two security men hustled him out of the hall, finally stopping at an office down the corridor. Ken sat against a desk. A female aide entered as the two security men left.

"Are you okay, Mr Mansell?" She asked. "A drink or something?"

Ken thought he could feel sweat, or was it blood, running down his face. "No! A toilet. I need to get…cleaned up?"

"The bathroom is there, Sir." The aide pointed to a door in the corner of the room.

Ken went to the bathroom and got sick before crashing to the floor, sat against the toilet. His mobile was already hot with messages and missed calls, but there was only one he wanted to answer at that point. Sharon picked up; she could hear the tears even though they were speaking over the phone. "Are you sure you are not hurt, honey?"

"I'm fine. I'm fine. Well physically, at least! Boris…and Kent…I saw…oh, my God. This is terrifying!"

"I know honey. I know. Look, you are safe. Dean and I will be with you shortly. I need to hug you."

This brought a smile to Ken's face, "Yes. Yes. I need you to hurry, please."

The call ended, but Ken remained on the floor against the toilet thinking. Sharon was ex-military and one of the first females to go behind lines in Eastern Europe and Asia during special operations. She was tough and he was just an administrator, a civil servant. Never had he expected to be in this position. Then his thoughts went to Roberts, '*Look after my family,*' he had said. Ken jumped to his feet and exited the toilet. Shouting to the female aide, Ken had a look of desperation on his face, "Jill is it? Roberts' family…they must be in danger, call the security services!"

Before the aide moved, the office door opened, Ken knew the man, M15 Commander, Josh Stirling. "Josh! I think the Roberts family is in danger…"

"We know, Ken." Stirling interrupted. We have agents on their way to meet his brother and family now. Calm down. Have a drink and let our people do their job."

Just over two hours had passed; Ken had been checked over and cleaned up as best they could. He had been waiting for Sharon; it was she that came through the door of the small office he was still in. They embraced and kissed. "Honey. It is good to see you!"

Sharon held the hug for some time before loosening her grip. "Are you sure you are okay?"

"Yes. I am fine."

Sharon looked her husband up and down; his words were not in sync with his body language. He was still shaken, probably still in shock. "What did the doctor say?"

"Shock but I'm with it now, honey."

"Did he prescribe whiskey?" Sharon smiled as she said this, looking at the half-empty glass and bottle on the desk beside her husband. The alcohol on his breath was also a giveaway.

"No just a couple. Seriously, I am all right and even better for seeing you." Ken gave his wife a peck on the lips to support this.

"Eh hmm!" Dean had entered the office.

"Hi, Dean. I am okay." Ken advised.

Dean took an empty glass and poured himself a whiskey before sitting on a couch near the window. "We have the Roberts family in protective custody. His brother Adam, has informed us that Roberts' wife and kids were taken hostage earlier today. He was abducted and taken at gunpoint to a road in North London." Hamilton took a few swigs of whiskey. "It appears that the terrorists were going to kill Roberts' family unless he took out the Home Secretary. His brother was the contact and pickup for the family after the news went out that the Home Secretary was dead."

Sharon's heart sank as she sat on the arm of a chair that Ken was now sitting on. "OMG. Poor Roberts."

Ken thoughtfully asked, "Did he have any option?"

Dean replied, "Maybe, maybe not, but in that situation, to protect your family, you would do anything…sorry guys." Dean knew that the Mansell's could not have children. A bullet wound a few years back had put a stop to Sharon's ability to have a child and indeed her military career.

Tears came to Sharon's eyes, "Don't be, Boss. That is history. The poor man. Roberts was a friend of ours. That may explain why he purposely missed Ken as the Home Secretary was his target?"

Ken was thinking hard, "So why shoot at me? Surely he knew the other security men would respond?"

"He had to give them time to react. They did and knowing Roberts would have a vest on and given the immediate danger they would have aimed at his head." Sharon was too aware of this protocol.

The door opened, and Jill spoke, "The brother and family are at our offices, and our team is at the house where they believe the Roberts were held."

"Sharon you go to the office, and I will visit the house." Dean noticed Ken's look, "Sorry, pal, but we need to work!"

Sharon kissed her husband, "I won't be long but go to bed."

---*---

Entering the lounge area in her office building, Sharon noted the woman on the couch cuddling her kids. Seeing an unknown man at the coffee machine, Sharon approached him. "Mr Roberts?"

"Yes. Adam Roberts. Sergeant Roberts' brother." Adam Roberts shook Sharon's hand.

"I am Agent Sharon Mansell of the WCST. We are a special government unit that ties worldwide security activities together in the wake of 9/11."

"Worldwide? What has my brother fallen into?"

Sharon poured herself a tea and sat at a chair away from the couch where the other Roberts family members were. Adam Roberts sat next to her." We are not sure yet, Sergeant Roberts. Ben, I knew him."

Adam took this in. "If you knew Ben, you will know he is…was a good man. He had no choice." Roberts pointed to his sister-in-law and nephew and niece.

"We know. There will be no comeback on Ben. Can you tell me any more about the kidnappers?"

Adam went quiet as he thought. "No, sorry. I have told your team everything. I was only involved around 6pm, but Esther and the family were abducted closer to 2pm."

"Ben's mobile showed calls from an unknown number a few times after 3pm. We believe they called him and met him to explain what he had to do. He did not start work until 5pm."

Adam thought further. "Why did he not call someone if he had that much time to prepare?"

Sharon moved uncomfortably in her chair. "These people are professionals and I am sure would have threatened his family not only today but also at any time after if Ben did not carry out their wishes. Did you speak to him?"

"No." A tear came to Adams' eyes. "I was abducted at gunpoint and led to Caledonian Road and told to obey the man or I and Ben's family were to be killed. Ben maybe a policeman but I am just a property surveyor. Anyway, when the time came, I sent the text as told but added, God be with you. I did not know what was going to happen but guessed it would not be good." Roberts paused. "The guy waited for about ten minutes then said something in a foreign language into his mobile and then said wait. I saw Esther and the kids come out of the house. They jumped in the car as the man got out and shouted go!"

Adam took a swig of coffee. "I hit the throttle and took off for a mile or two but eventually pulled up in that McDonalds' car park and called the police. While we waited, I turned on the radio, I did not know Ben was involved but put two and two together as the news was all over the radio. He killed the Home Secretary and the other guy?"

"Yes. I am so sorry. What language did the guy speak?"

"I don't know but little Suzie…" More tears came to Adams' eyes as he looked at his eight-year-old niece. "She said it was Russian. Apparently, her best friend at school is Russian, and she has picked up some words."

Sharon looked at the sleeping girl. "Thank you. Look, you and your family have been through a lot today, so we will let you rest. You are safe here."

"My wife. Your team said she is here, but we could not see her?"

"Of course. Yes, I will tell the team to let your wife in. I will see you in the morning." With that Sharon rose to leave, on her way out she advised another agent to let the wife in.

Sunday, December 7

Sharon had ignored at least three alarm calls; as a result, Alexa had a new, unofficial name, that it did not understand. Her mobile ringing could not be ignored. "Hi, Boss!"

"Sorry, Sharon but it is late!"

"It's a Sunday bugger off!" Ken shouted while turning over in the bed beside Sharon.

"Sorry. How is he?" Dean had heard the cry over the phone.

"He is fine and appears to have had a good sleep. Can I have an hour and then come in?"

"Yes. Of course. We're having a video conference call with our world colleagues, but I will fill you in when you arrive."

Sharon ended the call, stretched and got out of bed. Ken did not move. She asked Alexa to play the news whilst heading for the bathroom. Having washed and partly dressed, she came out of the bathroom. Alexa was not playing the news but Christmas jingles, Ken was sitting up in bed. "Why do I need the news? I was there!" Ken protested.

Sharon smiled, "No worries, honey." Sitting on the bed, she pulled her shoes on. As she went to put her shoulder holster on, she stopped. Ken did not usually take notice of this, but his look was of concern. "Sorry, honey, but it is my job."

"I know, honey. But…maybe we need to retire?"

"In our mid-thirties. Come on…" Sharon had realised what she was saying. "Sorry. No. Well, let me at least get the bastards and then maybe we can get an office job or something?"

"Mine is an office job!" Ken threw back at his wife.

Sharon giggled, "Sorry. Look, I will be careful, but I must do this." Pausing, she added, "Unless you need me home today?"

"No, I will survive. I will pop to the gym and maybe swim. You go catch the bastards!" With this, Ken leaned over and kissed his wife goodbye.

Sharon decided to drive the short journey, as Sunday traffic was always quiet. Sitting in her car, she also decided to listen to Christmas songs. One tune came on as she stopped at some traffic lights. It started to spin in her head until a loud horn disturbed her thoughts. Sharon thought of pulling her gun out to shut the inpatient driver up behind, but that was a little over the top. *Maybe,* she thought.

Arriving, she headed to her own office to catch up on emails and intel that she would not have seen overnight. For some reason, she turned the radio on in her office and listened to one of the songs, this time she found it on iTunes and played it a couple of times. "That's it!" She cried, even though she was alone. Hitting the internal code on her desk phone, she shouted, "Angie, you are there. Great! Come to my office, please." Her colleague was with her within a couple of minutes; Sharon wanted to share her thoughts. Having printed the words of a song, she wrote the first line on the whiteboard.

12 Drummers drumming

Then the second line.

11 Pipers piping

Circling the word *Drummers,* she drew an arrow to another box and wrote *Geneva* in it. Circling the word

Pipers, she again drew another line and box but wrote *Edinburgh* in it.

Angie got it and jumped to her feet and wrote the next line.

10 Lords a-leaping

Her line led to a box where she wrote the House of Lords. Both colleagues stood back and looked at the board to survey their work. Angie was first to scream, "You have it!"

Sharon smiled, "Maybe but it does fit. Wait!" Sharon thought further. "The 'Ho Ho Ho' messages do not tie as they have numbers that go up. One to three so far."

Angie said thoughtfully, "Are they just numbers of events? Today being four if we receive it?"

"So, by missing out the days of the atrocities, this suggests it will keep counting up to twelve? Fuck, does this mean there will be twelve atrocities? Nine more?"

Both women sat on the desk, taking in this possibility. "I hope not!" Angie said.

Sharon put her hands together in a praying clasp. "I pray not!" Pausing, Sharon added, "We need to tell someone fast. Get the boss here quickly, I will call Carl."

Carl answered Sharon's call quickly, "Hi Sharon. I am not in work for a few hours."

"Sorry, Carl but this is important. I think the Ho Ho Ho's are a count to twelve. Relating to the twelve days of Christmas song. I think there will be nine more attacks!"

"What?"

"Twelve Drummers drumming, Geneva. Eleven Pipers piping, Edinburgh. Ten Lords a Leaping, the House of Lords!"

"No. No, surely not!"

"If you receive a 'Ho Ho Ho 4' today then…Christ if I am right!" With this, Sharon turned and collapsed into a chair. "Oh, God, I hope I am wrong!"

Carl paused and thought. "Shit, Sharon if you are right then…no let me get to the office. I will watch for the four and maybe look at the song for some clues." With this, Carl hung up.

Dean entered the room following Angie. Sharon did not speak but looked at the whiteboard, Dean's eyes followed hers. "You really think this?"

"Yes. It fits and is too much of a coincidence. Drummers, Pipers, Lords." Sharon responded.

Dean paced up and down a few times, thinking. "It is crazy, but it is possible. What is the next line?"

"Nine Ladies Dancing," Angie replied.

Dean threw his hands up, "And that means what?" Sharon and Angie both looked perplexed and had no answer. Dean scratched his head. "Look we have not identified the bomber, and we are guessing at Zelse for Edinburgh and London. There doesn't appear to be a pattern, but this…maybe. Who have you told?"

"Just you and Carl," Sharon advised. "He will tell us if we get a 'Ho Ho Ho 4' today."

Dean gave a look of disbelief. "A possibility of nine more attacks. Please, God no!" Dean paused then added, "Angie, I want your team on this. Get the song words and analyse them. Now please!" Angie nodded a yes and left the room. Dean walked to the bar and poured a whiskey. "You want one?"

Sharon shook her head, "No, thank you. I will chase Carl."

Dean downed one immediately and already poured another. "I need strength to tell the PM and COBRA. Ask Carl his thoughts, especially regarding the Dancing Ladies."

"Ladies Dancing," Sharon froze realising she had stated the obvious without trying to offend her boss.

"Who cares? Keep in touch with Carl. I will talk to the Ministers and get back to you. It stays with the UK for now." With this, Dean left.

Sharon approached the whiteboard and wrote down the remaining song lines and started to put ideas next to them for the next few hours. *Three French Hens is easy, France!* Her concentration was broken when her mobile rang.

"Hi, Sharon, Carl." Carl paused, "'Ho Ho Ho 4' was just delivered."

Sharon's heart sunk. "So that bit is right, but it was easy. The song bit may not be. What are your thoughts on the Nine Ladies Dancing?"

"Moulin Rouge, Paris?"

Sharon was taken aback, "Wow, maybe. I thought the French Hens would be Paris?"

"Who knows?" Carl's whole demeanour spoke of exasperation.

"So, we need to warn the French?"

"Sorry, Sharon, you are the investigator. I will do what I'm told."

"Shit! I'll get back to you. Trace that bloody image!" Carl did not take this badly although Sharon had ended the call abruptly.

It was late in the evening and Dean had all his available staff working on the idea. He and Sharon had led all the activity throughout the day. "It's 11pm Sharon and we are no further!" Dean said in defeat as he looked at the tidied but still unclear view of the song and the links on the larger meeting room whiteboard. "We think there will be an attack tomorrow, but where?"

Sharon thought, "Don't be so hard on yourself, Boss. We are all doing our best. If we are right whoever is behind this is weird?"

"Weird? No, warped!" Dean added, "And even if we are correct about Ladies Dancing then where do we protect…is it just the UK or will they move abroad…Paris?"

"We need to involve others, Boss. They may not be able to answer this either, but we would be wrong if we don't?"

"And ties to the victims?"

"Again, so many dead. No, not yet."

"Go home to your husband. I will advise the French at least, brief the night shift and get some shuteye. And sorry, Sharon, I will pray tonight that you are wrong!

Monday, December 8

Having had a bad night's sleep and filled her husband in on her idea, the Mansell's were in the car heading for Downing Street for an 8am meeting with the Prime Minister. Upon arrival they were led to the cabinet room, joining those already seated Sharon sat next to Dean. "Agent Mansell, unfortunately, I think your idea holds water. Mr. Denton your views please?"

"Prime Minister the idea and information have been shared with all our security departments and the French. Unfortunately, we cannot ascertain when and where or even if another attack will happen."

"We have shared this with the French only?"

"Yes, Prime Minister."

"Anyone else have any thoughts?" The Prime Minister asked, looking around the table.

Philbin, the MI5 Director, replied, "We agree with the theory and have upped our efforts into finding the assassin, Zelse. I am happy to say the Russians are assisting. Is the key not to crack the image at GCHQ?"

General Buck moved uncomfortably in his chair before responding. "I have our best people at GCHQ looking at this, and…no we cannot solve this. Not yet, at least."

The Prime Minister looked critically at Dean, "Mr Hamilton, your unit has been set up for exactly this purpose."

Dean lowered his head. "I am sorry Prime Minister, even with all of our exhaustive ties we do not have a lead. We do have a few ideas on possible victim links, but it's too early to say."

"Then you must act in the…should I say…dark ways…to get something? Use the powers that the various governments have provided you."

"Yes, Prime Minister. Please remember we are not sure this is international yet."

"We have upped the UK security to its highest level and cancelled all leave for our security services, haven't we?"

Denton responded confidently, "Yes, Prime Minister." The meeting continued in a similar manner with Sharon noting that all the brains and all this power and the UK at least were fooled.

---*---

11pm and the clubs of Ibiza were packed mainly with young men and women, all tourists. No one took notice of the white delivery van driving down the street. The driver was making sure he did not break any minor traffic offences as he drove the van onto the seafront stopping for a minute. There were police but in low numbers, this was going to be easy. Downing the half bottle of Ouzo, he put the van in gear and accelerated off. About 100 metres later and at some speed he turned the wheel hard to the right. The van jumped the low kerb, hitting at least eight revellers on the pavement. People started screaming.

The driver ignored the screams and hit the throttle again, changing gear. The van smashed through the club's large window and ploughed through the young revellers sending people flying. Twenty metres into the building the van came to a stop having hit a water fountain feature. With the airbag deployed, the driver was safe. He could hear the screams of his victims. He looked through the door window and saw bodies and other people trying to run. Looking in the rear-view mirror, he saw more bodies behind him. He could hear the screams of the revellers even though the loud music was still playing.

He prayed for a moment. Looking up to the heavens, he leaned back and pulled the detonator. The explosion was loud and fierce, taking out virtually the whole structure of the club. The following fire was intense and spread fast, those that could not run were engulfed, as were adjoining clubs.

---*---

The Mansell's and Dean were in the WCST offices. The information analysis was still unresolved. Sharon was the first to note the BBC news feed from Ibiza:

Major terrorist attack in Ibiza. A van has driven into the dancing club, The Beat, followed by an explosion. Sources cannot confirm if this was a bomb or that the van may have hit a gas main. Firefighters are fighting a terrible fire at the club and surrounding buildings. The death toll is expected to rise into three figures...

Sharon started to cry as she looked at the screen. The scene looked horrendous. Ken went to his wife and hugged her. Dean spoke, "Look, we do not know if this is related?"

"Dancing Club?" Sharon stuttered.

"Not just ladies, unless it is a gay club?" Dean was despondent and meant what he had said.

"We don't know. I will talk with our Spanish colleagues now." Sharon made a few calls and eventually got hold of the WCST primary spokesperson. "Rocio please tell me about the club?"

"It is the most popular, having been refurbished just over a year ago."

"Is it a straight club? I mean men and women?"

"Yes. Full of young people."

"Did it have any special dancers or a troop of lady dancers?"

"Strange question, my friend, Sharon. Not specifically but there are modern pole dancers and some in cages of which most would be women."

"How many dead?" Sharon was tearful.

Rocio paused, "We have fifty-eight confirmed bodies. The fire is not fully out, and therefore, we cannot confirm further. Why are the UK interested, is it that many will be UK tourists?"

"Maybe. But no…" Sharon looked at Dean, who nodded. "We have an investigation going on here, and we think it may be linked. Can I send you some details and you send me back everything you can once you have it all together?"

"Yes, of course, my friend. It will be a few hours as we have some clearing up to do."

"Do you have any idea of who the terrorist is?"

"Not yet. You will be the first to know."

"God bless you all, Rocio. Our thoughts are with you and the people of Ibiza." With this, Sharon ended the call and could not help but cry. Ken hugged his wife closer.

Dean broke the silence, "Look we do not know it is linked but as the day, or at least the UK day has passed then maybe we should assume so. Go home and the night team will update us in the morning."

All three started to leave the room, at the door Dean asked, "The next clue?"

Sharon sniffled and replied, "Eight Maids-a-Milking."

Dean thought to himself, *Fuck, I hope all our brains can come up with something. We have what a day or so to stop whatever it is!*

Tuesday, December 9

"Honey I am off to Downing Street then COBRA. Do you need a lift?"

Sharon came from the bathroom. "No, honey, I will scooter to my office. Dean has called a worldwide conference call as we will be advising all WCST offices."

"Okay," Ken replied as he stood, he approached his wife and kissed her. "Catch you later."

Sharon took the electric scooter to her office; the fresh morning air gave her a feeling of freedom and a welcome break from the heartache she was feeling however, she could not help but stop and watch the screen in a breakfast café-bars' window:

"What is going on..." "Are these attacks linked..." "What are the security services doing to protect us..." "Where next..."

Sharon knew she had no answers, but she had to look.

Upon entering the office, she grabbed a tea and got straight into the mix of the team. All were having ideas. All were lost. The thoughts went from Wales to New Zealand to a thousand other places where cows were farmed. One idea was the Palace as it had maids. Sharon's head was pounding as she took a break at noon.

Her mobile rang and she put the phone to her ear, it was Carl. "Sharon. I have got help from Softdata, the biggest software company in the world!"

"Slow down, Carl. I know who Softdata is. All our computers work on it from home to work."

"That's it. Every computer and data centre in the world are Softdata, well virtually. Our systems at GCHQ and our colleagues across the world work off it so the image could be coming through the core code."

Sharon thought, "I don't have a clue what you are talking about, but will it find the location of the image?"

"I hope so. I need to talk to the major and get back to you. Fingers crossed!"

Sharon thought no more of this until Dean came back from the COBRA meeting around 4pm. "How was it?"

Hamilton shook his head, "Crap!"

"Sit, and I will get you a coffee?" Sharon made the coffee and went back to her boss. He looked a broken man sitting in the chair. "Are we getting the blame?"

"No. Not exactly but the PM wants answers and no one can give them." Taking a swig of his coffee, Dean paused to clear his head, "Have we got the details from Spain and any links?"

"Yes and no." Was Sharon's simple reply. "Carl had some good news earlier?"

Dean smiled, "Yes, I forgot. Do you have an overnight bag?"

Sharon smiled, "What?"

"We have agreed for Carl to go to Softdata's head office so as he gets direct help. And we want to send you with him as an agent involved in the case."

"Okay, but…"

Dean interrupted, "Are you needed here? Who knows? Will it stay in Europe? Look, we have some good people in the US, so maybe they can think differently."

"When do I leave?"

"Now."

"Wow. First-class I hope?"

Dean laughed, "No time for that, we have a couple of Typhoons waiting for you. With air-fuel refill, you will be there in about four hours!"

Sharon always held an overnight case in her office, and within the hour she had been helicoptered to a military base. Standing next to Carl she noticed he looked a little unnerved, "Your first time in a fighter jet Carl?"

Carl looked at the Typhoon in front of him. "What if I need to pee?"

Sharon laughed, "The pilot will tell you. See you there!" With that Sharon boarded her seat in the two-seater plane. A ground crew member helped her belt in, and with a thumbs up, she was ready. The pilot started to move the aircraft forward; Sharon could see Carl in the plane next to her that they were pulling away from. Even with the helmet and breathing mask on Sharon could guess that Carl was bricking it.

The plane taxied to the main runway, Sharon braced herself and the pilot lit it up. Sharon had not felt such power for some time, but even while gaining height at some speed, her thoughts were drawn back to her military days. Stabilizing she heard the pilot speak to her through the headphones, "I will let our friend catch us and then we are going to race." The pilot laughed, "We have a tenner bet on who lands first and an extra if we can make either of you sick!" The pilot continued to laugh.

Sharon giggled back, "I hope you have a couple of tenner's as you will lose at least one of those bets!" Sharon had never piloted before she but had been in many planes. She was confident she would not be sick. Although at the point where the craft hit supersonic, it took all her internal strength not to give in. *I wonder how Carl is doing,* she thought. With the incredible speed of the craft and a well-coordinated fuel refill, the plane was in place to land at a military airfield just outside Los Angeles. Sharon looked at the date and time details. Although leaving the UK around 6pm and taking into account the speed of the plane and time difference, they were in LA by 3pm the same day.

Sharon exited the plane gingerly and having been helped to the floor, walked towards her colleague's plane. Two ground crew were helping Carl who did not look good. "You okay?"

Carl looked at Sharon, "No. I need to clean up." Sharon turned to see the two pilots laughing and saw money changing hands.

Allowing Carl and Sharon to get their wits about them they were taken from the rest area to an office for an hour. "Hank Gibson. Long-time no see!" Sharon said as she smiled and then greeted her colleague with a hug. Hank was a big, Afro-American man in his late thirties with a warming smile.

"Hi, Sharon. Yeah, some two years? Excluding video calls." Hank returned the smile. "This the tech guy?"

Sharon turned to look at Carl. He had tidied up but still appeared a little lost. "Yes, Carl Hughes. One of our top techies."

Hank eyed up the shaking Carl, "Really!" He exclaimed while laughing. "So, we have been briefed already. Let's talk in the car."

All three sat in the back of a limo. "Ah, are we really off to Softdata's head office?" Carl asked excitedly.

"Yeah, about twenty minutes' drive. Ted Doors will see us."

Carl jumped in his seat, "We are meeting Ted Doors! The Ted Doors?"

"Yes. When the US government comes calling all respond," Hank chuckled.

"Sharon. Ted Doors, he is a God. No, the God!" Carl was on cloud nine.

Sharon laughed, "I know who he is. He founded Softdata and is the richest man in the world."

"I will kiss his fingers!" Carl was still losing it.

"Hey calm down, fella! Ted is human like the rest of us!" Hank continued to giggle. Only stopping when his cell bleeped.

Sharon noticed Hank's change in mood. "What is it?"

"'Ho Ho Ho 5 has been delivered," Hank said in a lower tone.

"Do you have any idea for the 8 Maids-a-Milking?"

"No, sorry, Sharon." Little more was said as the limo pulled up outside the swanky Softdata offices. Sharon, Carl, and Hank were led to the main office of Ted Doors. The female receptionist showing them the way knocked on the door before showing the three visitors in. Two men were in the office, both stood and walked towards their visitors.

"I am Ted Doors." The older but very well-groomed man said, holding out his hand to shake Hank's who was closest to him.

"Agent Gibson WCST. This is Agent Mansell and a GHCQ techie Carl." Sharon shook the extended hand of Doors.

Carl froze and for second or so left Doors' hand hanging. Coming to his senses, he took the hand and shook it vigorously. "Mr Doors…I am so honoured to meet you, Sir."

"You can let my hand go, please." Doors asked.

"Oh, sorry. So sorry!" Carl said, releasing Doors' hand.

"Thank you. This is Simon Dixon, one of my top tech guys. Please be seated. Would you like a drink?" Doors motioned to the receptionist who asked what drinks each wanted and went to a bar to make them.

All seated, Doors asked, "So how can we help our security forces?"

Hank replied, "You have been pre-advised about the Santa image?"

"Yes, we have."

"Then we need to find where it is coming from?"

"Okay. May I know why?"

"Why do you ask?" Hank asked.

"I am just trying to understand the importance of this. Thank you, Leanne," Leanne, the receptionist, had provided the drinks.

Sharon took a sip of her tea. "Very important. We believe it may have a link to recent terrorist acts in Europe."

Doors thought, "I see then it is of the utmost importance. We at Softdata will fully support you. I, of course, started the company and the original code; however, things move on and now I spend more time running the company than coding. Simon here is one of our newest coders. He will assist you directly."

"Thank you, Mr Doors," Hank replied. "Carl here will spend time with him. I have no idea about computers," Hank ended with a giggle.

"Of course, you would not." Doors also giggled. "Simon, please."

Dixon stood and gestured to Carl. "Mr Hughes, please join me as I will show you our coding room and team."

Carl could not believe his ears. "Oh my God, really. Yes, please." Carl stood as he spoke.

Dixon said his goodbyes and led Carl out of the office. Sharon could not but note that Carl was like a kid in a sweet shop. "While your colleague is working, would you two like a small tour of the premises? We have a little museum of our works here that could be of interest?"

With a "Yes" from both Hank and Sharon, they joined Leanne for a private tour without Doors.

It was 10pm; Hank and Sharon had been at the hotel for about half an hour when Carl joined them smiling from ear to ear. Carl sat next to his colleagues at the bar and couldn't keep the excitement out of his voice, "Someone pinch me…no don't I'm in heaven and don't want it to stop if it's a dream!"

Hank laughed, "So you enjoyed it?"

"OMG the hardware, the speed, the brains. I thought I understood code, but wow these guys are phenomenal!"

"That is all good; however, did it go anywhere?" Sharon was getting tired.

"Give me a minute, Sharon. I've been to the Holy Grail of IT!"

Sharon giggled, "Okay, that is great. But get to business, I am shattered."

Carl had forgotten to be tired but understood his colleague. "No, not yet but…we are definitely a little closer. Tomorrow will be better. I am learning so much!"

"Then let's call it a night." Sharon ended the evening.

Wednesday, December 10

10am, and the three colleagues were in the hotel restaurant finishing breakfast. Dixon walked into the restaurant and greeted them in turn. Turning specifically to Carl, he said. "Carl. You were impressive yesterday."

Carl smiled, "Thank you. More, please?"

Dixon laughed, "We need to heighten the level today, so we will not be going to the office."

Carl was intrigued, "Where then?"

"We will be visiting Mr Nazrith." With this, Carl jumped to his feet and punched the air screaming with excitement without realising everyone in the restaurant was looking at him.

Dixon smiled, "Shall we go?"

With all four behind the privacy windows of the limo, Sharon decided she needed to know more. "Mr Nazrith?"

"OMG, Sharon, you are so…out of date!" Carl stopped himself from swearing. "Steve Nazrith is the real brains behind Softdata now. He got involved a few years after Doors started the company, but the rumour is Nazrith took it forward and made it the most useable software in the world." Carl looked at Dixon for reassurance.

Dixon nodded his lead. "That is correct. Mr Nazrith is considered our chief coder and Mr Doors right-hand man. Both are geniuses."

"Okay, so he does not work at the Softdata offices?" Sharon asked.

"Let me!" Hank had something to say, "Sharon. Steve Nazrith was injured in a terrible car crash some six years ago and has been an effective recluse over the last few years. He is wheelchair-bound."

"Oh!" Is all Sharon could say.

Dixon added. "That is correct, although recluse is a bit too harsh. Mr Nazrith has all the modern facilities he requires at home and thankfully his mind and specifically his fingers are un-effected, so his work continues." Little more was said as the limo pulled off the highway onto a short drive. The gates opened electronically, and the limo came to a stop twenty metres from the house. All exited the car and Sharon looked around. The house appeared a single story, but they had been driving along the coast so must be on a cliff. As they approached the large doors, they opened electronically sliding sideways. A woman dressed in a nurse's uniform approached the guests. Sharon noted the woman looked older than she had first thought, there were signs of cosmetic surgery.

"Welcome to you all. Mr Nazrith will see you now. Please follow me." Upon walking through the large doors and into a very short hallway, Sharon could not believe her eyes. Although it was a very large room, she was looking at a wall full of windows that overlooked the sea. *Wow!* she thought.

"Our guests. Please give Mr Nazrith a minute." Sharon noted a man had approached them. "I am Mr Yates, Mr Nazrith's assistant. Would you like some drinks?" All declined the offer of drinks.

Carl was beaming and moved towards some paintings on the wall. "Wow, guys! These paintings are actual code…this one uses binary to make up the picture." Walking a bit further, he screamed, "OMG, this is a notebook with handwritten code and notes." Carl was looking at a notebook inside a glass case on a cabinet below the paintings.

"Those are my notes. In fact, my first ever when working with Ted." Carl looked around; Nazrith had entered the room, gliding towards them in a high-tech electric wheelchair.

"Mr Nazrith. I am so…so honoured to meet you." Carl was the first to go to shake Nazrith's hand.

Hank approached Nazrith, "You have a beautiful home, Mr Nazrith!"

Nazrith smiled and shook Hank's hand, "Thank you. And your young lady?"

Sharon smiled and approached Nazrith. Even in the wheelchair, he looked suave, well shaven, and immaculately dressed. *Mid-fifties*, she thought as she shook Nazareth's hand. "Agent Sharon Mansell WCTS. A pleasure, Mr Nazrith."

"You two are British?" Nazrith smiled.

"Yes. English actually!" Carl just wanted to talk.

"And Gibson, you are our government?"

"Stars and stripes, Mr Nazrith. LA local."

"Good." Nazrith paused. "I suggest you take Kevin's offer of a drink as Mr Hughes here and I will need some time together. Mr Hughes, shall we find that Santa?"

Carl's smile nearly broke his face, "Yes, Sir. Mr Nazrith!" With that, Carl followed Nazrith to a side room.

Sharon and Hank took their drinks, lemonade of some sort and headed for the veranda that ran the length of the windows. It was sunny, warm and with a light breeze, the house was on the side of a cliff and had floors below them. "Forget the IT stuff. This place is heaven!"

"As I said, it is beautiful," Hank responded to Sharon.

Sharon sat on a sun lounger; Hank next to her. "I have not heard anything from my team taking us forward," Sharon said as she took off her light jacket and kicked off her shoes to enjoy the setting.

"Ours neither," Hank leaned back on the lounger and sipped his lemonade. "The Spanish have the name of the van bomber, Estefan Cortes. He is known to us."

"Yes. I have heard of him. He was with ETA?"

"That's right. But it is not their type of work. We are looking for his bank accounts and any allies. We also believe Zelse is in France."

"You have her whereabouts?"

"Not exactly but again give it time."

"We don't have much time. How crazy is this? Here we are sunning ourselves when we know somewhere in the world an atrocity will happen."

Hank thought, "I know, but there are hundreds of our team around the world working on this not to mention the CIA, FBI, and even the KGB!"

"They gave us Zelse's whereabouts?"

"Vanchenkin owes me a favour."

Sharon laughed. "Hey, we are all WCST, Chenks should be telling me!"

Hank laughed. "He has, you just aren't reading all the intel."

"All this effort and no one has a clue. 8 Maids-a-Milking?"

"The three French Hens is easy. France will be a popular place for us guys in a few weeks. The Golden Rings have got to be the Olympics?"

"Too easy and besides this is not an Olympics' year."

"Their HQ in Lausanne maybe?"

"Switzerland again?"

"Maybe not."

Sharon changed tact, "Do you think it is religiously based?"

"Who knows? It is an obvious link, but Zelse is not a religious terrorist. Although money is to be worshipped!" Hank said and aloud himself a giggle.

"No. There must be a link. We have to look deeper."

The conversation went on for over an hour, both so engrossed they missed Carl approaching them. "Hey, guys. That was the most awesome hour of my life!"

"So please tell me you have something?" Sharon wanted to know.

"Not exactly but we have cracked some of the stem code…"

"English, please!" Hank interrupted.

Carl rubbed his chin. "We have a direction that I think will lead somewhere."

"Lunch break over. Get back there and find our Santa!" Sharon pushed.

"I can't. Mr Nazrith can only concentrate for short periods. He needs an hour or so rest before we will get back to it."

Hank kicked off his shoes, "Then let's enjoy the scenery!"

---*---

John Grisham was a larger than life character, a Californian milk billionaire. He and his beautiful wife Vanessa exited their Rolls Royce outside Merced County Hall. The Milk Federation's Christmas event was the place to be and show off. Grisham wore all white with gold trappings. Jewellery rolled off Vanessa. The couple entered the hall, shaking as many hands as possible or kissing cheeks as required. Finally, inside the hall, they approached the main stage. On the stage was a table with eight chairs facing the hall; the Gresham's were the last to approach the stage.

"Their wives look younger every year," Vanessa Grisham whispered to her husband.

Grisham looked at the three seated men and their wives next to them and sniggered. "Hell, Tomsy's is hardly out of college. But don't worry dear, you are a little older but more beautiful and classier than anyone of them." Grisham kissed his wife.

Mike Dragin, the event organiser, welcomed the Gresham's to the stage and showed them to their seats. Once Grisham had stood to start his speech, Dragin left the stage. He was walking along the side of the hall towards the doors at the back, some distance from the stage. Dragin looked back at the stage, Grisham was still addressing the crowd. *Four billionaires and their trophy wives and here he was nearly in bankruptcy due to his second divorce,* he thought to himself.

Standing by the door, he took a deep breath. *This was payday,* he reassured himself. Taking the few steps to be just outside the door, he looked at Grisham and the large papier-mâché cow that was behind the stage. Dragin looked around, all eyes were on the stage.

Removing a cell phone from his pocket, he entered a code then jumped behind the wall to his left.

The blast was big and the doors he was standing in front of came off their hinges, one hitting his leg. Screaming in pain, he stood and started to hobble toward the outer doors. Within a metre of the outside doors, two cops came running in.

"What is it?" Dragin screamed.

"Mr Dragin. We don't know?" The first cop shouted, "You are injured. Let's get you out of here!" With that, the cop and his colleague helped Dragin out of the building. They did not notice the wry smile on Dragin's face.

Thursday, December 11

It was less than an hour's travel to Merced County. Upon arrival Hank and Sharon exited the car. Ducking under the police tape, Hank approached a police officer. "Morning. Who is in charge?"

"Captain Henson. Over there in the suit," the officer pointed.

Sharon followed Hank, they stopped beside the captain. Sharon looked at the damage to the county hall. Both large front doors were hanging off their hinges and the roof had caved in. Firefighters had finally managed to control the fire an hour or so before their arrival. "Morning, Captain. What is the situation?" Hank asked, flashing his WCST ID.

"Good morning, Sir. They had no chance, thirty-two dead and forty in hospital…some critical."

"Anything to go on?" Sharon asked.

Henson looked at Sharon and Sharon flashed her ID. "Not yet, ma'am. Our forensics team are on the case. A local explosion, so the bomber is either dead or was close when it went off."

Hanson asked, "We will have a look around. You will pass all the details to us?"

"Yes, Sir. Please get the mother fuck that did this!"

Hank smiled and touched Hanson's arm, then headed towards the building. He and Sharon did not speak but took in the damage. Fireman allowed them to enter the site. Sharon noted how bad the damage was first through the front doors then looking into the hall, *they had no chance* she could not help thinking. Walking around the remnants of the building both spoke to the forensic officers; it was too early to have anything. Hank and Sharon left the hall after about half an hour. Noticing a coffee van parked there for the varied emergency forces staff present, Hank headed to the van. Coffee in hand he went to speak but stopped as his mobile beeped. Hank looked at his mobile screen, shook his head and showed the message to Sharon. 'Ho Ho Ho 6' had been delivered. Sharon sipped her coffee, she preferred tea, but coffee was all that was available. Leaning against the back of the van, she sighed. "This is crazy Hank. We have all the world's security forces to hand and we have no idea who is behind this!"

Hank shook his head. "We have never experienced anything like this. Four different countries and what would appear to be different factions carrying out the atrocities."

Sharon thought, "There has to be a link…" Sharon stopped to answer her mobile. "Hi, honey. How are you…"

Hank moved away from Sharon to give her time to speak to her husband alone. *Swans a-swimming* was going through his head. *Hell,* he thought, *the motherfuckers are giving us a clue and yet we have no idea.* Noting Sharon ending her call, Hank asked, "How is Ken?"

"He is fine. My team and government have no more than you have." Sharon paused, "Swans?"

Hank grimaced, "I was thinking that. The UK again, the Queen's swans?"

Sharon thought. "Maybe. We must find Zelse or trace Cortes' money. I'll call the boss and push them along!"

Early afternoon and Sharon and Hank were in the local police station. Secure access was possible through the secured network. Sharon checked her emails, *nothing!*

Sharon used the phone, "Hi Carl. Anything?"

"Hi Sharon. No. We get close, but then it moves."

"Come on you are with the best brain in the business, you must have something!"

Carl paused, "Hey, we are doing our best. That Dixon guy is here as well with Nazrith and I. We can't do anymore!"

"Sorry Carl. I know. But something is going to happen in the next twenty-four hours and we are stumped. Useless even."

Friday, December 12

Hannah Zorgas was completing her concert in a beautiful Athens hall; it was around 10pm Greek time. Her Husband Del Font stood at the side of the stage, watching his beautiful wife playing the Lyre. He took a swig of his water, loosening his throat having just sung three songs with his wife. Hannah finished with a flurry and the audience took to their feet, clapping and cheering in appreciation. Del put down his water and took to the stage. The audience screamed louder and clapped faster. Del Font was a much bigger star than his wife, world-renowned. Del walked towards his wife with a big smile on his face. He was so proud of her. As he approached her, he gave her a lingering kiss. The audience roared with approval. The hall was noisy and everyone on his or her feet. The two men coming from the back of the stage were hardly noticed.

Del caught them out of the corner of his eye having released his wife. His look to his security staff was enough for them to head towards the two men.

As the security guards got close to the two men, both men smiled, then chanted. Both men pulled out an MP5 from under their coat. The first round of fire took out the approaching security guards. One man then started to fire into the wings. The other approached Font and Zorgas. Del yelled, "Run, Hannah!" as he pushed his wife aside and placed himself between the gunmen and her. Before he could fully grapple the gunmen, he took ten shots to his body and hit the stage floor. Hannah froze as she saw her husband hit the floor in a pool of blood. She caught the eyes of the gunmen some five metres from her, as she turned to run the bullets ripped through her back.

---*---

Sharon sunk in her chair as her Greek colleague, Eleonora, briefed her. Hank was by Sharon's side with a whiskey in hand watching the TV. The news was full of the murder of Del Font, one of the biggest music stars in the world and his wife, Hannah Zorgas.

Sharon finished the call and addressed Hank. "Both gunmen have escaped. Thirteen dead and many injured. There was at least a third gang member who was waiting in the getaway van. He was in a stolen police van. The police van has been found, but no clues yet."

Hank looked up, "Fuck!" he screamed as he threw his half-empty glass at the wall, watching it break into many pieces.

Sharon ignored this and stood to pour two whiskeys, giving one to Hank. Both downed their drinks in one. "Athens?" Is all Hank could shout.

Sharon sat back down. "The time difference, it was the 12th in Athens. There must be a link. Look can we get back to your office? I need more computing and communications power?"

"Yes. Let's go!"

Saturday, December 13

The morning had been full of many meetings and phone calls. Lunch missed; Hank entered the central control room. Standing on a raised area, he looked down at his staff all busying themselves on phones, PC's or at whiteboards. Catching a glimpse of Sharon, he signalled a drink motion. Sharon noted the action and joined Hank in the small café area.

"You really throw yourself into things!" Hank noted.

"I have to. My brain is buzzing so I need to think or be challenged."

"Anything?"

"The Spanish have traced some of the money to Cortes. Well, at least they found out two million pounds was paid to his brother. He is with the Spanish WCST and they are trying to piece things together. But it does appear as though Cortes gained the cash somehow and left it in a case for his brother to find, having text the details of where it was minutes before he killed himself and the others."

"Do they think his brother is *not* involved?"

"Unfortunately, yes. At this point."

"You said pounds?"

Sharon thought about it, "Sorry euros."

"That is a hell of a lot of money."

Sharon nodded her head in agreement. "We have some ideas on future clues. Watch!" With this, Sharon walked to a whiteboard and drew.

Geese—No!

Gold rings—Olympics?

Lausanne, Switzerland...hit?

Athens, Greece...hit,

Rome maybe?

Calling birds—??

French hens—Paris.

Turtledoves—Rome?

Partridge/Peartree?

Hank noted, "A couple of Rome's in there?"

"So far, we have not had the same country twice."

"And people links?" Sharon again drew on the whiteboard.

Drummers—no obvious target

Pipers—no obvious target

Lords—British Home Secretary

Ibiza—no obvious target

California—four billionaires??

Athens—Font and wife, target?

Zelse—Cortes???

Sharon had just about given up, she couldn't see anything of use at all, "We have nothing!"

Hank stated the obvious, "Geese is the next one."

"If there is a link between here and the next atrocity then Canadian geese, or, this time of the year they are in Mexico?"

"So, all we can do is heighten security in nearly every major city on Earth!" Hank stated in disbelief.

"Carl is getting somewhere, but Nazrith has to keep stopping due to bad health. They thought they had a link to an IP address in Rome but lost it."

"Rome again?"

Sharon thought, "Yes. I need a plane!"

Hank laughed, "Rome. It could be anywhere?"

"We believe Zelse is still in France or at least was, so at least I am closer to her."

"You taking Carl…" Gibson's mobile answered with a beep and a message.

Ho Ho Ho - 7!

Sunday, December 14

Sharon was on another military jet within the hour, making the lone trip to Rome. Exiting the plane onto another military landing strip, Sharon jumped into a waiting car. She was alone in the back seat of the vehicle. The car took off; Sharon waited a few minutes then spoke to the driver. "Hi. What date and time is it?"

"December 14th, 10am, Mrs Mansell."

"Thank you…sorry I did not get your name?"

"Titus. Ma'am. Agent Justus Bannic will be at the office when we arrive there in about half hour."

"Thank you." With this, Sharon kicked off her shoes and made herself more comfortable across the seat. She recalled Justus, a younger, dark-skinned handsome agent, *oh those Italians, oops I'm married!* Sharon thought. Opening her laptop, she studied the picture of the whiteboard she had written in

California the previous day. *Arts* Sharon thought, *Drummers, Pipers, Singers.* She looked at an email from Eleanora.

Greek tradition Swan plays Lyre—*Having drawn the strings over its shell, Hermes, the protector of shepherds, made the first Lyre. He presented it to Apollo, who gave him a winged warder in exchange…*

Wow! is it really this cryptic…but it did tie Swans to the Lyre to Athens…Geese and music. Is music the connection?

---*---

The small aircraft was approaching Kariba Airport, Zimbabwe. It was 11am and a lovely bright morning. As he called through to the control tower he smiled, he enjoyed his job. "Papa twenty-three requests landing permission?"

The radio responded, "Landing permission granted. You know the way Nelson." Nelson smiled to himself, his friend Mosi was in the control tower. Nelson manoeuvred the plane into position and started the descent. Landing gear already down there was 100 metres before touchdown. Nelson was thinking of his little girl's birthday the next day.

Having been on a two-week world tour of flight duties he was happy to be home.

Monitoring the runway approach, Nelson caught a flash out the corner of his eye. Moving his head to the left to see what caused the light, he screamed in terror. Nelson had no chance to avoid the missile that, upon impact, blew the aircraft apart.

Mosi stood from his chair, having witnessed the plane explode in mid-air. The wreckage was already all over the runway. Mosi fell to his knees and cried.

---*---

"What! Turn the radio up!" Sharon shouted to Titus. Titus turned the radio up; he had been listening to the English news for Sharon's benefit.

Reports are coming in of a plane crash in Zimbabwe at Kariba Airport. Casualty numbers are not known as yet, but eyewitnesses suggest it was shot out of the sky by a missile.

Sharon thought, "What day and time is it in Zimbabwe?"

Titus considered his answer before he spoke. "I believe we are on the same time zone as here. It is the 14th..." looking at the clock on the dashboard he continued, "...11.15am. We will arrive in five minutes." Sharon collected her bits. upon exiting the car. Agent Justus Bannic approached her.

"Sharon, it is a pleasure to see you again." With this, Justus placed a kiss on each of Sharon's cheeks.

"Hi Justus. Is the Zimbabwe airplane our case?"

Justus froze before replying. "In many ways, I hope so as I do not want a bigger atrocity today. If you can count sixteen dead as a small atrocity."

"Sixteen...definitely a missile?"

"Yes. A small anti-tank missile launcher has been found already."

"Prisoners?"

"No. The two assailants getaway truck did not start. The armed Zimbabwe police shot them dead in the gun battle."

As Sharon entered the WCST building, she added. "Well, at least we will know who they are."

Sharon was led to a café area and offered drinks and rest, which she took advantage of. Some two hours later she walked into Justus' office. "Sorry Justus. A couple of long hard fights in a few days takes it out of you."

Justus smiled, "Of course. This is my Superior, Antonio Cryce."

"Hi Antonio," Sharon said as she held out her hand.

Cryce shook her hand, "Agent Mansell. And how is Dean?"

"He is good, Sir."

"Good. We had a few wines together on a course only a few months ago. Dean said he would send his best man." Cryce looked Sharon up and down, "Certainly not a man!"

Sharon smirked, "No, definitely not. Justus, what do we know?"

Justus smirked, "No change. Sixteen dead with their plane shot down by a missile."

"Shit!" Sharon thought, "Oops sorry, Sir!"

Cryce laughed, "I would agree with you. We have men at the apartment where the terrorists were staying. The locals knew one of them. Once we have something, we will share it."

"Quick work. Is there anyone we know on the plane or the…terrorists as you call them?"

Justus replied, "No. We have the names of all, but none stand out. The two dead terrorists, Bello and Kalu, are ex Somalian terrorists but more recently mercenaries."

"More money!" Sharon said aloud. Justus looked at Cryce, who shrugged his shoulders.

"What the hell has this to do with Switzerland or Edinburgh?"

"Sharon, we are all at a loss." Justus tried to be reassuring.

Sharon thought, "Look. If this is today's attack then we have…about thirty-six hours to think what and more importantly, where the next one will be. The gold rings?"

"We have security all over Rome. Especially the Coliseum and the Pantheon to name a couple…" Cryce paused. "Do you think it really is Rome?"

"Who knows? May I have a room and a whiteboard of my own please?"

"Yes, of course. Give me five minutes." With that, Cryce left the room.

"Straight into it?"

"Yes!" Sharon got to work, after catching up on her emails and a quick call to her husband she attacked the whiteboard.

Geese, Kariba Airport, music Font, no Lyre…

All was going through her mind while scribbling on the board.

The Olympics must be Lausanne.

Sharon called Sara, her Swiss colleague. "Sara is there anything going on tomorrow in Lausanne. Any major Olympic event there or anywhere in the world? Even a Christmas party?" Sharon was full of questions, but there were no answers. Ending the call and taking a tea break, she was back at the whiteboard. *No wait, it can't be?* One of her favourite films is the Wild Geese and it ends with a plane crash at Kariba Airport. *It must be! Is our terrorist a film fanatic? Gold rings…wait…Goldfinger…Fort Knox…* Sharon's thoughts were all over the place but some of it seemed to make sense.

Her workings were interrupted as Justus entered the room. "Sharon. I am going across the road for a pizza. You hungry?"

"Yes. Hawaiian if you don't mind and some garlic bread…oh and prawn toast…is that Italian?" Justus laughed, he realised he had interrupted Sharon in full thought mode. Exiting he returned a half-hour later with pizza and sides. Sharon dug into the food, but her mind was still thinking. Justus watched for an hour, not talking just watching as Sharon wrote more onto the whiteboard. "That's it. Matthew, Mark, Luke, and John. Yes! It has to be!" Sharon shouted out loud in a eureka moment.

Justus looked up, "And?"

"No! No! Don't disturb me. Wait!" With this Sharon hit the keyboard, typing madly, checking the internet. Finally, she sat back and said, "There!" Pointing to her screen. Justus stood up and walked behind Sharon to look over her shoulder.

Between 1558 and 1829, Roman Catholics in England were forbidden from openly practicing their religion. In order to inculcate the catechism in their children, Catholics created the song as, basically, a series of mnemonic devices to give kids the broad outline of the Roman Catholic worldview and teachings.

Adding to the whiteboard she wrote:

The partridge in a pear tree represents Jesus (is a bird that'll sacrifice its life to save its children)—it is Christmas!

Two turtledoves represent the Old and New Testaments

—or True love, who?

Three French hens are faith, hope, and love

—Paris!

Four calling birds are the Gospels of Matthew, Mark, Luke, and John

—*the Vatican!*

Five golden rings are the Pentateuch, the first five books of the Old Testament

— *Olympics?*

Six days of creation (geese a-laying)

—*No Wild Geese film, Kariba Airport!*

Seven gifts of the Holy Spirit (swans-a-swimming)

—*Swan, Lyre Athens!*

Eight Beatitudes (maids a-milking)

—*California milkmen!*

Nine fruits of the holy spirit (ladies dancing)

—*Ibiza!*

Ten commandments (lords a-leaping)

—*London, Home Secretary, Arts Secretary!*

Eleven faithful apostles (pipers piping)

—*Edinburgh!*

Twelve points of belief in the Apostle's Creed (drummers drumming)

—*Geneva, UN, bankers?*

Justus read the notes and said aloud, "The writings of a madwoman!"

Sharon pushed Justus aside. "I know. But I bet you the Vatican one is right. And it seems to be leading to someone…a true love? But who?" Sharon walked around the office, only stopping to pour some lukewarm water to make a cup of tea. "Who do you know at the Vatican?"

"You are serious?"

"Yes. OMG, do you think they are after the Pope?"

Justus thought, "Come on, Sharon. We can't run around scaring the Pope…what on a whim?" Sharon gave Justus a stare. Finishing off his drink he said, "Okay. Okay. Let me talk to someone." With this, he left.

Returning an hour later, Justus approached the sleeping Sharon at the desk. Jabbing her arm, Sharon woke. "I will have Titus take you to the hotel. The Vatican security has accepted your theory and is searching the palace. His Holiness is guarded very closely. Go and get some proper sleep."

Sharon did not wish to argue and soon found herself in a hotel room near the Vatican. Picking up her mobile, she called her husband to both update him and to say she loved him.

Monday, December 15

Sharon woke, getting out of bed she went to the window and drew back the curtains. The sunlight provided a feeling of warmth; the sight of the Vatican provided hope. Sharon showered and dressed then checked her phone messages before going for breakfast. Sitting at the breakfast table she placed her laptop on the table and checked her emails. Carl's email was fascinating.

We thought we had them but no. Then we got London, and then we lost the trace. They are good! Ho Ho Ho 8 is expected today. Like your ramblings, defo the Vatican. Music connection or maybe an art connection.

Sharon thought further on this, but again Justus interrupted her thoughts. "Morning Sharon. We are going to church. The church!"

"Morning Justus. Will the main man be there?"

Justus chuckled, "Yes, but he will be hidden. Let's go!"

Within the hour, Justus and Sharon were entering the Vatican. Standing in the main foyer, Sharon noted at least four Swiss guards present, all in their splendid uniform. A tall man dressed in a dark suit approached, taking Justus' hand first the man introduced himself. "I am Enzo Cargli, the Vatican Chief of Security."

"Agents Justus Bannic and Sharon Mansell of the WCST. We have met before."

Cargli studied Justus, "Ah yes! Sorry, Mr Bannic. We have indeed." Cargli then looked at Sharon. "We have not. Welcome to the Vatican. Please follow me." Sharon and Justus followed Cargli through a couple of corridors and finally into a small office. Cargli sat and motioned for his guests to sit. "Although we have many threats to his Holiness, few come via the WCST. We have been looking, in-depth, into your theory and we have a concern with a new food delivery driver."

"Quick work…" Justus threw in, "…highlighting this driver so quickly?"

Cargli looked uneasy then added. "Only just. It would appear that Mr Rarb has delivered…let's say some food with a little more bang to it."

Sharon was taken aback. "You mean explosives?"

Cargli fidgeted in his chair. "Yes." He responded quietly.

Justus looked at Sharon and then addressed Cargli. "You have a bomb here, now?"

Cargli smirked. "It is in an area just to the side of the delivery yard. We believe Rarb blocked the CCTV with his van and was able to drop off explosives and a weapon in an old kitchen larder that is used for storage nowadays but rarely entered."

Sharon thought, "So Rarb knows the layout?"

Cargli stood and walked to a window. "No. We think he is just the delivery driver and the goods are there for someone internal to pick up and use."

Justus was catching on, "So, who knows the room is there. Is it locked or just not used?"

"We have our suspicions."

"And these suspicions are not to be shared?" Sharon quizzed.

Cargli turned to look at Sharon. "No, we are just unsure. There is obviously an insider and well…I am not sure who we can trust."

"How do we progress this?"

"Rarb is expected with another food delivery this afternoon. I thought a hidden WCST presence might capture him and his accomplice."

"Hidden with some explosives?" Sharon asked.

"I doubt if they are primed. But yes. Please."

Justus replied, "When and how?"

Cargli sat against the window ledge. "Today. If you leave now through the general exit, I will leave in ten minutes then meet you near Caeduccies. There is an alley around the back. I will put you in the boot of my car then return here via a private entrance and I can get you into the larder unseen."

Sharon looked at Justus and then addressed Cargli. "You really cannot trust anyone here?"

"Of course, there are people here I trust, but…if someone has approved Rarb's work ID…and someone hid the explosives after Rarb left…I do not think he was ever alone long enough to do all of that by himself."

"And we have to trust you?"

Cargli was taken aback by Justus. Cargli pointed to a gold cross on his desk. "Trust the almighty. I would die to protect his Holiness." With this, Cargli made the sign of the cross.

A half-hour later and Justus looked and saw the plain-looking car reverse into the alleyway. Justus looked at Sharon. "Are you ready?" Sharon nodded in response and both got into the boot as it was opened by the driver. Justus pulled it shut. As he pulled the lid shut his mobile beeped.

'Ho Ho Ho 8' was delivered.

The drive was short and Sharon could tell by the voices that the driver was being challenged but only briefly. Sharon gripped her gun as the boot opened. Cargli placed his finger to his lips and pointed to his left. Justus got out first and went through the door that was being pointed to, Sharon followed. Once inside, Cargli led them through smaller dark corridors which Sharon assumed were secret passages that would have been used to hide from marauders in the past. Eventually the three came to a door. Cargli pulled a key and unlocked it. "This is the internal door to the larder. Once you are inside, Rarb should enter from the other side. Whoever comes through this door afterwards will be my traitor." No more was said and Justus and Sharon entered, taking cover on either side of the darkroom.

A short time passed and the front door opened, shedding light into the larder. Sharon looked at Justus; both had their weapons drawn. A man entered the larder through the door, carrying a small box. Sharon watched as the man walked towards a cupboard, stopped and placed the box he was carrying onto a shelf next to the cupboard. As the man turned to leave, Justus moved. Catching up behind the man, he placed his arm around his shoulder then putting his hand over the man's mouth as he flicked him around. The man turned only to be looking straight into the barrel of Sharon's gun held to his head. Sharon made a shush motion to her lips. Justus taped the man's mouth and then his arms from behind. Looking around, Justus saw a large corner cupboard to his left and led the man to the area. Sharon closed the front door just as she heard the internal door lock being unlocked. Sharon took cover. Justus had his gun to the first man's head. The internal door opened and a man entered. Looking around the room, he walked towards the cupboard. Noticing the box, he went to pick it up. Sharon moved first, jumping from cover, weapon drawn. "Freeze! Police! I will shoot!"

The man froze. Justus pushed his man into the room, gun still at his head. The second man asked, "Who are you?"

"We are the Police working on behalf of Cargli. Who are you?" The man started to turn, "Arms up!

Do not move...answer me!" The man prayed in his head briefly then went for the gun in his jacket. Sharon responded and two shots hit the man in his torso. Justus fired two further shots. The man fell to the floor.

Sharon heard cries and footsteps coming towards the room. She looked at Justus. Justus put his gun on the floor and held his arms up. Sharon copied. Four Swiss guards entered the larder, weapons drawn. Taking in the sight of two people holding their arms aloft and another taped up, they noticed the body on the floor. The first guard raised his gun at Sharon. Sharon shouted, "Police. Call Cargli!"

The guard looked at his superior on the floor, looked back at Sharon and placed his gun centimetres from her face. "Hold your fire!" Came the cry as Cargli entered the room. "Holster your weapons. All of you!" The four guards turned to see their superior, each looked at each other confused. All four holstered their weapons as Cargli ordered again, "Holster your weapons!" Sharon wiped her brow. Cargli walked to the body on the floor, bending over he turned the body over. Making a cross above the body, he stood and spoke to Sharon. "Are you okay?"

"Yes. Who is this?"

"Anelli Felloni, our Chief of Staff. Did you have to kill him?"

Justus spoke, "I am sorry, Sir. He drew his weapon. Whether he was to shoot us or the explosives, we were not taking the chance!"

Cargli thought. "Of course. Guards this is to be kept secret for now. Call Lucas as he has explosives training. Move Anelli's body onto that table. Justus, Sharon and Rarb come with me."

A short time after, Sharon and Justus found themselves in a custody area below the Vatican. Cargli had ordered two guards to un-tape and frisk Rarb before he addressed him. "I know you have been dropping explosives here. The box today was the remote detonator. Who were you and Anelli in with?" Rarb ignored the question. Cargli walked around a few steps, gave a quick look at Justus then stood face to face with Rarb. "These people may be the police or the government. They may even abide by the rules. I however, answer to someone much higher and you are in his building threatening his life. Talk, or I will have my guards gain the information required."

Sweat ran down Rarb's face. He looked at Justus, Justus looked away. "Mr Cargli. I will not deny that I am the delivery driver of the bomb; however, I swear that that is all. I have no idea of the plot or who is behind this."

Cargli moved away from Rarb. "Make me believe you." As Cargli finished, the door opened and two

Swiss guards entered the room and stood next to Rarb.

Rarb dropped to his knees and with tears, he pleaded. "I swear I only dealt with Anelli. He contacted me and he paid me."

Cargli looked at Justus. Justus spoke, "Where did you get the explosives from?"

"The Metal Man on the border."

Justus knew this was the name of a known smuggler. "Then you will help my team capture the Metal Man at least, if not who is behind this planned outrage." Rarb nodded, still kneeling.

Cargli thought, then addressed Justus. "You two may leave and we will keep our friend here until at least the morning. We will hand him over to help capture the black-market man you speak of."

Sharon went to speak, but Justus raised his hand before addressing Cargli. "Yes Sir. I will send my men tomorrow morning, but you must promise me you will provide any information you gather."

"Yes, of course. Guards, lock Rarb up for now." With that, the two guards pulled Rarb to his feet and dragged him out of the room. Sharon could hear Rarb crying for mercy.

Within the hour, Justus and Sharon were in the hotel. Justus ordered two drinks from the bar then joined Sharon sitting at a table. "Rarb is scared of the Vatican guard. Surely they would not break the law?"

Justus swigged his beer. "The Vatican is a separate country and well…the Knights Templar and all that. Rarb will speak if he knows anything."

"Good!" was all Sharon could reply.

Tuesday, December 16

Sharon had had a good night's sleep before she entered Justus' office in the centre of Rome. Catching the clock just after 8am, she sat on the windowsill looking over the city waiting for Justus.

---*---

Across the world, a wedding party was well on its way with revellers drinking and dancing hard. The bride, having changed into a white party dress, looked out across the New York skyline. Lost in thought, here she was a small-town teacher who found and fell in love with a millionaire. Her wedding day was ending, but looking back into the room, she was happy. She could see her family and friends celebrating her big day at one of the most expensive rooftop wedding venues in the world. Father Condal approached her. "It was a lovely wedding, Miss Katie...I mean, Mrs Bartlet."

Katie smiled, "Yes. Thank you Father. Your sermon was very religious and full of warmth."

Father Condal smiled, "Yes, I enjoy weddings." Pausing for a moment, he continued, "Of course lovely couples such as yourselves inviting me to the party afterward is always an extra benefit."

"Oh, Father. I am sure you guys can let your hair down sometimes. Besides you are *the* priest here!"

Father Condal laughed, "Yes. I have been here for many years. I feel like Elvis having my own show." Katie and Condal both laughed aloud. Katie smiled upon seeing her wonderful new husband approach her…it was her last thought as the room exploded.

---*---

Justus entered his office and without saying a word to Sharon, he turned the TV on to a news channel. Sharon moved closer to the screen taking in the report. "OMG a fire in New York on what…a skyscraper at a wedding?"

Justus replied, "Yes. That is what is being reported; however, our sources suggest a bomb."

Sharon thought, "The poor couple." She dropped her head slightly and asked, "Is this related to our events?"

"Well it is the second day, an even number plus…five Gold Rings. A wedding?"

"Yes. Who were the couple?"

"A New York millionaire, Ross Bartlet, and Katie Pann, his bride. Ross is the son of Jack Bartlet, the property magnet."

Sharon thought. "I will call my team. We need the guest list and to start looking for ties between this couple and any of the other atrocities!"

Sharon spent the remainder of the day catching up on calls and intel with colleagues all over the world, only catching a ten-minute call with her husband to lift her spirit briefly. 3pm and Justus had arranged a conference call. Regardless of the time in the world, the screens were filled with WCST agents, all ready to relay their information. An hour into the call and all appeared despondent; no one could make a connection. Sara from Switzerland spoke, "'Ho Ho Ho 9" was delivered. Carl anything from Softdata?"

Carl was on one screen next to Hank. "No. I am sorry, but even with the brains of Softdata, we cannot locate where it is coming from."

Hank spoke, "Colleagues, we are at a dead end. Six atrocities and one stopped but no links."

Sara addressed Hank directly. "Hank, we are in this together. Do we have any news on Cortes or Zelse?"

"No, but we do believe she is in France," Helga interjected.

Hank spoke, "And you are ready for her on Saturday. We all think that is France. Paris, maybe?"

Anton Lamure, the French WCST agent, spoke. "Yes, of course. We are all hoping that Sharon is right and we have at least stopped the attack in Rome tomorrow. The Vatican is secure Justus?"

"Yes. It is in lockdown. His Holiness has a Christmas event tomorrow afternoon. Our prisoner has at least confirmed that was the target for his bomb."

Sara closed her eyes, then opened them, "Thank God we have saved that atrocity. The Pope and in the Vatican…that is beyond belief. Does your prisoner know any more?"

"No, he was just the equipment provider. Anelli Felloni was the planner and probably the one who was to explode the bomb. We have found lots of money in his family's account. With this and Cortes, can we not find the source?" Justus could not help but smile at his Swiss colleague.

Sara gave an embarrassed smile, "We are the best bankers in the world, but we do not have all the money in the world. Besides what has been traced so far appears to be large amounts of cash payments that bounce between various online banks. None of the people in the different countries where the money was originally banked have been identified."

Sharon spoke, "So if I and others are right there will be no attack tomorrow?"

Hank was the first to reply, "Probably not. All of these attacks have been planned for months and I doubt that different planning could be made at such short notice. Besides I am sure no one will get near the Vatican tomorrow."

Justus responded, "The Vatican is safe, but would our foe have a backup…" Even Justus dropped his head slightly, noting a similar reaction from his colleagues.

Dean spoke, "Continue swapping intel, ideas, whatever. We must get this or these terrorists!" Sharon and her colleagues continued into the evening, looking for links.

Wednesday, December 17

Sharon exited the hotel dialling her husband, "Hi Honey. How are you?"

"I am good, dear. Are you guys any more forward?"

"No. I am so embarrassed. All the anti-terrorist teams in the world and we cannot find a lead."

"You saved the Pope?"

"Yes. That is the only positive. I am off to Paris. Basically, all the world's security will be there for Saturday."

"It's a big place. Look, I was playing that CD by the poor musician killed in Athens. Hannah Zorgas and recalled something."

"What?"

"She is...or was, rumoured to be the illegitimate daughter of Kent the Arts Minister that was killed with Boris."

"Really. How do you know?"

Ken chuckled, "I live with these people every working day, so you pick things up."

Sharon thought, "I'll get my team onto it. I am sorry, but I need to rush. Love you! See you soon!" As Sharon got into the car, her mobile beeped, 'Ho Ho Ho 10' had arrived. A tear came to her eye.

Booking into her hotel a short flight and a few hours later, Sharon immediately went to shower, knowing she had a meeting with her French colleague Anton Lamure a little later. Having showered she went to the steamed-up mirror, but before wiping it, she thought and wrote.

Kent Arts, Hannah daughter. Boris not target, Pope not target?

There was not enough mirror space to write any more. Sharon thought, *Maybe the targets were not the main ones. Maybe the secondary or not as important targets were the actual targets. That's it! Give me a whiteboard and I will link these.* Dressing quickly, she called her lift.

Upon entering the WCST Paris office Sharon met Anton with the standard European welcome, kissing his cheeks on either side. "Is this place closed down?"

"Yes. Well, as much as we can. We have help from all our colleagues. Even your boss, Hamilton, is here!"

"Okay." Sharon looked at her friend, slightly older and a little fatter since they had last met. "The beard?"

Anton chuckled, "The trend. I hear your husband has one as well?"

Sharon also chuckled, "Middle-aged…well, nearly middle-aged men, trying to look modern."

Anton laughed, "And if you say I am getting fat, I will kill you!" Anton was still smiling.

Sharon laughed, "I was not thinking that. Shall we get working my friend?" Dean said hello but sat overlooking the team of agents busying away before him. He smirked as he could see Sharon scribbling over a large whiteboard with three French colleagues taking in her every word.

Anton spoke, "Sharon is good. She has something, but there are many secondary targets as she suggests?"

Dean smiled, "Yes, I know. But we have little else." Work for the day completed Dean was at the hotel bar with Sharon. "Drink this you deserve it."

"Thanks, Boss!" Sharon said as she kicked off her shoes and snuggled into the chair, sipping the wine. "Wine in Paris, there are little other pleasures in the world than this!"

Dean giggled, "I agree. It is awful sitting here being useless and people dying all around us. At least tomorrow will not have an atrocity?"

"I do hope so."

"Are we any closer?"

"No…not really. We do not believe it's a terrorist or a joint terrorist plan or one organization. Maybe an individual. There are too many dead and too many possible links. I need to sleep." With this Sharon said goodnight and went to her room.

Thursday, December 18

Cardinal Lott had just left the hotel having had breakfast with his American friends in a posh Rome hotel. It was just after 11am and he was to ride to the Christmas event at the Vatican. Walking towards the car, his driver was already opening the rear door for him. The Cardinal bowed his head to his driver as he approached him. A motorbike came from nowhere, hitting the Cardinal's driver as it pulled up beside the Cardinal on the pavement. The Cardinal froze and looked at the helmeted rider, the rider pulled out a gun and emptied three bullets into the Cardinal's head before pocketing the weapon and turning the throttle to escape on the motorbike as quick as it had arrived.

---*---

Sharon shouted, "Bastards!" As she took in the news from Justus over the phone. "You think Cardinal Lott is related to our case?"

"Probably. Cardinal Lott was to attend the Vatican event and would have been killed by the planned bomb!"

"Yes. To keep on time our foe has had to improvise. I mean the killing of just the direct target and not an atrocity or others?" Sharon was thinking aloud.

Titus thought, "Yes, this would be a replacement atrocity. This means our foe is now improvising and will make mistakes."

Sharon thought and responded. "Maybe. It fits the MO. We would all think his Holiness would be the target and Cardinal Lott would be just one of the others. But if this is correct, then this suggests something or will give us a lead."

"I will get everything we have on him to you. Plus, I have spoken to Hank, as Lott was American. Good luck!" Sharon put her mobile down on the desk, took a deep breath and went to work jumping from laptop to whiteboard. Going into deep investigation mode and thought when the files on Cardinal Lott arrived.

Lott…American Cardinal…Arts Minister…daughter…religion…

While Sharon was working away, she was unaware of what was going on less than five miles from her.

---*---

Zelse was unhappy. Her life was organised and planned. To pull a job forward, especially by twenty-four hours, did not make her happy. Her driver had chosen not to talk; upsetting the world's best assassin was not a good idea. "You have my back up in place? My escape plan?"

"Yes, Miss Zelse!"

"My targets are all in place?"

"Yes. Our insider has them in the back bar having afternoon drinks." Zelse shook her head. She had never failed a job and would not do so today.

---*---

Sharon jumped back from her desk. *No...It can't be.* She thought. She stood and looked at the whiteboard again.

Suspected paedophile...Lott...rumours...in America...years ago.

I need to read more, what were the allegations?...wait a priest was killed in the New York bomb...?

---*---

Zelse exited the taxi, dressed in an expensive black bodycon dress with expensive add-ons including a designer handbag. She was not questioned as she approached the hotel door. The doorman smiled at the attractive, classy looking lady as the automatic doors opened. "Good afternoon, Miss."

Zelse smiled back and continued to walk towards the bar area. *No visible sign of police, good!* She thought.

---*---

Rumours…choirboys…

Sharon thought as she took in the various articles in front of her. *Wait! Stop!* Sharon pulled back to an old photo of a choir with Priest Lott at the front. Below the choir boys' picture their names were printed. A name had caught her eye and she needed to take this in more. Reading the name three times, she stopped to clear her head. Reading it a fourth, she shouted aloud…

---*---

Zelse entered the bar area, the large garden doors to her right and the three women targets to her left. Zelse walked up to the three seated women. The first stopped talking and looked up at her. "Can I help you?" Zelse smiled and removed the revolver from her bag; three shots and three dead women lay in front of her. Each shot in the head. *Oh! I am so good!* she thought as she turned. Everyone around her was already running. Zelse pulled up her dress revealing tight shorts and ran to the doors that led to the garden. Exiting the hotel, she caught the motorbike coming from her right. As the bike stopped beside her, she jumped on, holding the rider around the waist tightly as he turned the throttle for the escape.

---*---

"Nazrith!" Sharon screamed as she jumped to her feet. Everyone in the office also jumped with shock at the excited movement of their colleague. Sharon held up a pad and repeated, "Nazrith! I think it is him!"

Dean was the first to her side. "Sharon, please! What are you saying?" Sharon took a deep breath and went to the whiteboard and wrote on the whiteboard.

Lott paedophile the US…Father Condal married NY…

Bartlet and Pann…married Meredith Morgan to Nazrith!

Dean looked at the board, "Are you saying Nazrith is behind this?"

Before Sharon could answer an agent called from the side of the room, "Sir!" Anton looked towards his agent who sat in front of a large screen.

Ho Ho Ho—10½

Got me now?

Dean spoke first, "Sharon explain yourself!" With this, he and Anton were by Sharon's side.

"As a young boy, Steve Nazrith was in Cardinal Lott's choir, when Cardinal Lott was still a priest. More recently there have been allegations around Lott being a paedophile but being a Cardinal, he appears to be protected or at least innocent until proven guilty." Sharon paused. "Anyway, the priest killed in New York is the priest who married Nazrith and his last wife, Meredith, at the skyscraper rooftop place in New York. Arts Secretary Kent, although now divorced, married Nazrith's first wife, Kate McLeod. Basically, he stole her from Nazrith."

"And the others?" Anton said aloud.

"Fuck the others!" Dean was very blunt. "Get me a phone we need to arrest Nazrith at least!"

"Sir!" The same agent called again catching the three's attention. "We have a shooting here in Paris just now…"

Anton interrupted, "What do you mean…nothing is expected today…or has it already happened?"

"Initial reports three women, three shots. It could be Zelse?" The agent advised.

Anton thought, "The three women?"

Dean thought, "You guys look at that. Sharon…Nazrith…Carl…!"

"I'm on it!" Sharon was already calling Carl's mobile.

Carl answered. "Hi, Sharon!"

Sharon asked, "Carl, are you okay?"

There was a short silence as Carl looked to his side; Yates had a gun to his head. "The 10½ message came from…here!"

"No, Carl. Please tell me you are okay?" Before Carl could respond, his mobile was pulled from him by Yates and handed to Nazrith.

"Mrs Mansell you messed with my plans. However, this was not unexpected; therefore, I have just brought Plan B into play."

"You bastard. Do not touch Carl!"

"Ha, ha, ha!" Nazrith sniggered. "Do you think I care about him when I have already killed my previous treacherous lovers?"

"Look, Nazrith, we can talk? I know about Cardinal Lott!" Sharon thought playing for time would work as she could tell Dean was already getting hold of Hank.

Nazrith's tone changed. "Sick pervert. He started all the bad things in my life. I should have killed him a long time ago. Anyway, thank you for the fun and I hope when you put it all together, you will understand. But for now, I need to hide." With this, the phone call ended.

"I have got a hold of Hank. He will have men at Nazrith's shortly!" Dean advised.

Sharon held her mobile to her chest, "I hope so!" Sharon and Dean sat to await the news from the US, and twenty minutes later, they had it.

Hank was on the phone to Dean. "I am sorry, Dean. We are at Nazrith's mansion, but he has gone and so far there's no sign of Carl…apart from his broken mobile. We will do all we can to find him!" Dean ended the call and relayed the message to Sharon, giving her a quick hug to comfort her; Carl was a friend and not just a colleague.

One hour later and with still no news of Carl, Anton approached Sharon and Dean who were sitting drinking a tea and a coffee. "The three dead are Nazrith's previous wives. Apparently, he had got them all to Paris under the illusion that he was to meet them as a reunion and probably give them more money."

"Money!" Sharon shouted. "Just because you have billions, it should not allow you to have so many people killed!"

Dean gave Sharon another hug. "We are looking for Carl. Think positive." Turning to Anton, he asked, "Then if it was Zelse, are there any leads?"

"Maybe. It would appear today's attack was rushed and we have a lead on one of Zelse's accomplices. We have agents and police near his place now and we think he is not alone."

Sharon spoke, "Until we hear of Carl I want to work. If Zelse is found, then I want to be part of it!"

Anton looked at Dean and then addressed Sharon. "Yes, of course. Let us confirm what we think and then we will act."

Sharon picked up her mobile to answer her husband. "Hi Honey. Your report on Nazrith is obviously true. He has been behind this all along."

Sharon smiled. The voice of her husband brought warmth. "Yes. I have put together some of the killings to the song and him but not all. Anyway, he admitted it on the phone. He has Carl."

Ken thought, "I know honey. I hope he is okay. Hank has a good team and I am sure they will find him. I hear the three wives are dead?"

"Yes. Confirmed. We may have Zelse."

Ken paused. "Wow. She is one hell of a prize if you do get her."

Sharon saw Anton entering the room, looking very excited. "Look, honey, I need to go. I Love you!"

Anton was with Sharon and Dean. "It is Zelse. She is shacked up in an apartment about ten minutes from here. It is under surveillance. Let's go. You can suit up in the van." With that, Sharon and Dean followed Anton out of the office to a police van. During the short drive, both Sharon and Dean put on bulletproof vests and police helmets. Sharon liked the MI6's provided. The van pulled up in a side street. The vans' lights were off. All three exited the van quietly; thankfully, it was now dark in Paris. Anton led them to an armed police Inspector. "What is the situation, Jacque?"

"Mr Lamure. Can you see that apartment block just down there? Third on the left and the top apartment on the third floor?" Seeing Anton nod, he continued. "That is Henry John's apartment. We have him as the driver of the taxi Zelse got out of before the killings. Our men caught him on a roadside CCTV camera outside the hotel when fleeing. Simple mistakes when rushed." The Inspector paused. "Anyway, our thermal imaging suggests three people are in the apartment. One female. We have men on the roof to see if we can get a microphone in."

"And the other apartments?"

"We have quietly emptied them all. Do you and your team wish to join me in the apartment below Zelse?"

"Yes," was the reply from all three. They followed the Inspector into the shadows.

The special forces team was on the roof. Moving quietly, they were to take up positions to jump through the windows of the apartment below. Lines were being attached for this. An officer moved along the edge. There was no roof void because of the flat roof, half of which was a roof garden. As the officer walked past one chimney a bird flew out of the stack being woken by his presence, startling him.

Inside the apartment John, one of Zelse's accomplices heard the noise above. Zelse had come from the bedroom. "Was that on the roof?"

"Yes! A bird, maybe?"

Zelse walked to a window and tweaked open the blind to look out. "It is too dark!"

"Meaning?"

"Is there a power cut? The streetlights are out."

"No. We have lights." Duchamp, the other occupant, had entered the main room.

Zelse thought, "Get the weapons I am going to have a look!" With that, the three armed themselves with M16s and headed for the door. Zelse exited first and looked over the dark staircase to the floor below. *Too quiet,* she thought. Pointing upwards Duchamp followed her signal and headed up the stairs to the roof. All three waited at the roof's door while Duchamp pushed it open. There was garden furniture, storage boxes and chimneys in his sight.

The police hidden on the roof aimed…waiting for the order to shoot. John moved out from the door first…something glinted to his left on the moonlit roof. John raised his weapon, the policeman with the sight on his rifle panicked, jumping to his feet, he called, "Police stop!"

John responded with a round of bullets putting the policeman back on the floor. Duchamp went to head back down the stairs but saw torchlight heading his way. "Shit!" Zelse screamed as she exited the roof door gun blazing but immediately turning to her right and heading away from John and the crackle of gunfire coming from the police. John hit the floor under a flurry of gunfire. Duchamp had turned to follow Zelse, both ran while emptying spurts of gunfire towards the pursuing police.

"Shit they rumbled us!" Anton shouted as he broke cover looking up at the roof and the blaze of gunfire above them.

Zelse took the three-metre jump from her apartment roof to the next with ease. Duchamp joined her but stopped and hid behind a small wall on the next roof. Smiling at Zelse, he said, "Go, my friend. You are the master, and the cause needs you. I will buy you time." As Zelse smiled in response, Duchamp looked above the wall and emptied more bullets at the police on the other roof.

Sharon took in the action above her and called, "Dean, Anton this way. The other building." Both Dean and Anton responded by following the sprinting Sharon along the road, in the opposite direction to where they had been heading,

Zelse could hear the gunfire behind and upon seeing the top of the fire escape took to the ladder. The short metal ladder took her to metal stairs that she ran down at pace missing every other step, Zelse jumped to the alley floor below. As she stood to run, three people came running around the top of the alley. Zelse opened fire downing at least one figure. Sharon had reacted first and jumped behind a waste bin. Looking up, she could see the fallen Anton with Dean near him but also behind a container. Sharon nodded and Dean knew what to do. Looking out from his cover he fired some shots in Zelse's direction. Zelse, brazenly was still standing where she had stopped and returned fire in the direction of the bullets coming her way. As Dean pulled back, Sharon broke cover and opened fire, each shot hitting Zelse and she fell to the ground. Sharon approached the body on the floor, keeping her gun still raised. "She is dead! How is Anton?" Sharon shouted to her colleague, although still watching Zelse's lifeless body.

"He is hit but alive!" As Dean shouted, more police came running around the corner to assist.

Friday, December 19

Sharon sat where she had slept on a bench in the hospital corridor. Dean approached with a cup of tea. "Good morning Sharon. Any news?"

As he said this, a doctor headed towards them. "Agents Hamilton and Mansell, your colleague Anton Lamure is okay."

Both Sharon and Dean gave a sigh of relief. "The operations went well? Can we see him?"

"Yes, the operation was successful. Thankfully the full SWAT suit he had on took the bulk of the bullets. The only head wound does not appear to have entered in any depth. Most others grazed him. But he has multiple shots in his arms and top of his legs and he lost a lot of blood. He needs to rest, so maybe in a few hours?"

"Thank you," Dean replied as he sat next to Sharon.

"That is good news," Sharon stated as she scoured her mobile in between sips of tea for any update on Carl.

Dean jumped slightly as his mobile rang. "Hello. Hank, what is the news?"

"Hi, Dean. Nazrith is in his private jet heading from California to Washington we believe. He has Carl and Dale Teldove and Roman Italo the husbands of his last two wife's hostage on the plane."

"How?" Dean asked, having put his mobile on speaker for Sharon to hear.

"Similar to the wives. It would appear he secretly asked them to meet him in LA to make up with them. Paying all their expenses, they were here a day or so together. While the shootings were going on in Paris, the husbands were abducted. Only now we know where and by whom."

"Why Washington?" Sharon asked.

Hank paused, "He knows the president and we think he will wish to see him personally. As if *that* is gonna happen."

---*---

Dove sat in the seat looking out of the jet's window. Usually, such a ride would be first-class and therefore enjoyable; however, this time, he was sat at gunpoint with two other hostages. Nazrith had been praying whilst sat in his wheelchair in the corner of the specially adapted jet.

Dove spoke to him and Nazrith smiled before turning his wheelchair around and heading to his three passengers. "You have killed them all. My wife. You mad bastard!" Italo accused Nazrith. Nazrith looked at Yates who had the gun raised at his three captives and smiled. "Why?" Italo asked through tears.

Nazrith laughed, "Oh, I don't know…or maybe simply because they dumped me. Especially Meredith, who left me just after my accident and when I was imprisoned in this wheelchair. And you two fucks took them!"

Carl spoke up, "Mr Nazrith, what is your plan now. For us?"

"Still the polite one…Mr Nazrith, I like that." Nazrith circled in his wheelchair. "You are an excellent coder and I had to work hard in stopping you from finding me."

"I was sitting next to you most of the time."

"Yes. Keep your friends close and your enemies closer!" Nazrith laughed again.

"I am not your enemy but a fan. I still see you in awe. You are the greatest programmer in the world…if not ever."

"Thank you. That will help my decision on whether to kill you or not."

"And us two?" Dove asked.

"Oh! You two are dead; it is just a matter of when." Nazrith laughed.

Dove went to stand and Yates placed the gun to his temple. Another armed guard pointed his weapon to the other seated hostages. "Do you wish to die right now?" Yates asked, Dove sat back in his chair.

"The White House, Mr Nazrith?" Carl was trying to calm the situation down.

"I know the president. I wish to make a plea to him directly. You know I am the victim here." Nazrith said with a sarcastic smile.

Carl paused, "Yes, of course. You said something about that priest. No one should go through that. I am sure my employers will listen; they have power too."

"What are those?" Italo asked, catching sight of the two fighter jets near them.

Yates spoke, "We have an escort to Washington Dulles airport. Have a drink, we will be landing shortly."

---*---

"Get a better angle!" Dean shouted into the microphone. He and Sharon had moved to the WCST Paris office and were looking at a large screen showing the approaching plane about to land at Dulles. Sharon watched as the plane landed and taxied behind several armoured vehicles along the runway.

Hank was looking at a monitor still in LA. "Dulles has a remote area exactly for this type of incident. The plane will be led there just in case there is any trouble."

"Is the president going to meet Nazrith?" Dean asked.

Hank paused, "No. Our job is to take Nazrith out. Whenever we feel there will be fewer victims.

Especially Carl and co." Sharon's heart sunk at this point. She had full respect for her US colleagues, but she knew deep down the protection of their president and people would come above that of Carl and the other hostages.

"Ah, we are here. Mr President has said he would meet me. Is that not nice?" Carl could sense that Nazrith was still being sarcastic. Nazrith moved along the plane, looking out of the windows. He could see police and military everywhere. Turning, he approached his newest wife, his nurse. "Dearest. Please take the envelope I gave you. You will go out first and speak with the authorities." Pamela smiled at Nazrith then went to a drawer and removed an envelope. Returning to her husband, she placed a kiss on his lips. Nazrith smiled and nodded to the pilot who had joined them. The pilot opened the aircraft door. Pamela looked at Nazrith, then walked out of the plane and took the ten steps down onto the tarmac. Two FBI Agents emerged from behind one of the vehicles and headed towards her. Pamela met them some fifteen metres from the aircraft steps.

Pamela gave the envelope to the male agent. "These are Mr Nazrith's documents for the president. Will they meet here or at the White House?"

The female FBI replied, "Not yet, Mrs Nazrith. We will need to talk to Mr Nazrith first."

Pamela replied, "Oh!" Then placed her arms behind her back.

Carl was watching from one of the aircraft's windows and noted Nazrith had turned to look at him and the other two hostages. Nazrith said, "Gentleman. Yes. It is simple. This is all about revenge."

Carl noted Nazrith was perspiring, small beads of sweat were running down his forehead. Carl screamed, "No!" Nazrith pulled a cord from below his wheelchair.

---*---

Sharon screamed at the monitor as she saw the airplane explode into a ball of fire. "Carl!" Is all she could scream as she collapsed back into a chair. Dean looked at the screen, then went to Sharon's side and held her hand.

Hank's voice came through the screen speakers. "The mother-fucker. I'm sorry guys, but it is unlikely anyone has got out apart from Mrs Nazrith." Sharon and Dean did not respond and they both watched the monitor in silence. The fire service was already dowsing the burning aircraft. Ten minutes later the plane was smouldering and the flames and smoke were sparse. It was clear that the aircraft was severely damaged. *No one could survive this,* Sharon thought.

It took a further hour before Sharon got the news she already knew. Hank spoke through the monitor. "I am so sorry, my friends. There are no survivors." With that, Sharon stood and exited the room for some air.

Dean followed Sharon out five minutes later. "Are you okay, Sharon?"

"I did not expect that…suicide I mean…I thought the bastard was arrogant enough to have tried it with the president at least?"

Dean thought, "Obviously not. But he got the last two men that took his wives."

Sharon thought, "Two turtle doves. No?"

"Remember one was named Dove."

"Fuck! It is so obvious now!"

"You call your husband. I will check on what is happening. We will need to talk about Carl and organise the recovery of his body and bringing it home. I need to arrange to get us home as well." With this Dean hugged Sharon and went back into the building.

"Hi Honey."

"Sharon, love. Are you okay?"

"I am fine, but Carl was on the plane."

Ken paused, "Yeah. I know. I am so sorry; he was a great guy."

"Yes. A geek…" Sharon allowed herself a chuckle as she recalled her friend. "…but a funny, nice guy."

Ken chuckled, "Yes, he was. When are you coming home…or should I come out to you?"

"No. Dean is arranging transport and I should be home shortly. I will go back in and pick up some detail then text you. I love you, hun. See you soon. Kiss. Kiss!"

Saturday, December 20

Sharon had cried herself to sleep, having arrived home around four in the morning. Now awake, she rose and put on a dressing gown, then walked to the kitchen of her flat. Ken, seeing his wife, smiled. Giving her a big hug, he said, "Good morning, honey."

"Morning…" Sharon looked at the clock. "You mean good afternoon."

Ken chuckled, "You needed that sleep. Sit on the terrace, it is surprisingly warm. I will bring you brunch."

Sharon walked to the terrace and sat on a chair. Ken was right, for a late December day the sun was up and it was comfortable if not warm. Sharon looked out over the Thames as she sat in silence, thinking of her lost friend, Carl. "Do you think it is all over now?" Ken asked as he placed the food and drinks onto the table and sat next to Sharon.

"I hope so. He appears to have got everyone."

"Disturbed bastard!"

Sharon thought before replying. "Yes. No matter what happened to him, he cannot be forgiven for all the deaths he has caused over the last few weeks."

"The partridge in a pear tree?" Ken asked as he smiled.

Sharon jolted up. "Yes. Shit maybe there is more…"

"Slow down!" Ken grabbed her arm as he said this.

"What? Has something happened?"

"No. But I believe we have the answer. Pamela Nazrith is under house arrest in Nazrith's Washington apartment on the exclusive Pear Tree estate."

Sharon paused, "He had that planned all along. He was never going to survive?"

"That's your job to figure out," Ken chuckled.

"Yes. But it can wait. You need to spoil me today and tomorrow at least. More toast please."

Monday, December 22

Sharon exited the car at the military airfield. As she walked towards the military plane that had just landed, she was joined by Dean at her side. About twenty metres from the rear of the craft, they stopped and watched as the back of the aircraft opened and lowered into a ramp. After waiting a few minutes six uniformed soldiers exited the aircraft carrying a coffin. A seventh soldier leading the squad approached Sharon and Dean, the coffin bearers stopping behind him.

"Do you wish to see inside the coffin now, ma'am?"

Sharon replied, "No. Not now." She then walked to the front of the coffin, kissed her fingers, and placed them on the coffin. *Welcome home friend, I will see you in a minute.* Sharon moved aside and the soldiers marched on. The leading soldier stopped and turned going back to Sharon.

"Sorry, ma'am, I forgot. This has been checked." With this, he gave Sharon an envelope. He then followed his troop.

"What is that?" Dean asked. Sharon looked at the envelope. The outer envelope had the seal of the US president on it although it wasn't sealed. Sharon pulled another envelope out from the inside. She froze upon seeing the Softdata logo. Sharon looked at the envelope and read the writing on the front of it, then pushed it into Dean's hand. "I am not reading that bastard's note!"

Dean held the envelope and read aloud the note where the address would typically be. "*For Agent Mansell. Please read this. My story is to be known.* It is signed by Nazrith." Dean looked inside, "There is a letter inside. It looks quite long. I am not reading this. You should read it."

Sharon grimaced, "Okay, in a while!" Taking the envelope, she put it in her pocket. Taking a short walk, Sharon entered a hanger, Sharon stopped. Greeting and hugging Mrs Hughes and Mr Hughes, who planted a kiss on her cheek. "We will have Carl moved to wherever you wish. The force will make all the arrangements for his funeral. Your son was a respected agent and a good friend to many."

Mrs Hughes returned the hug, "Thank you, Sharon. Ralph and I will think of what is best and we will let you know." With that, the Hughes left the hanger, shaking Deans' hand as they went.

Dean looked around the big empty hanger, apart from the coffin which alone in the middle on a stand. "It is a shame it is locked. Once the undertakers do what they do, I am sure they will kiss their son again." Tears came to Sharon's eyes as she sat on a chair next to the coffin. "You need to read the letter."

Sharon looked up at Dean. "Yes. Give me some time."

"Of course." Dean placed a reassuring hand on Sharon's shoulder then left her alone in the hanger.

Opening the envelope, she removed the handwritten letter. She looked at the coffin for a moment and then started to read,

Dear Mrs Mansell, Sharon!

Although we only met very briefly, I felt that you would be the person to tell my story. I have a lot of time for the Brits and of course a good-looking woman. Many people would have been envious of my life until that tragic day of the car crash. The crash removed many of my abilities, such as walking and took the life of my son. You cannot imagine not only the physical pain but also the mental pain that followed. I had everything until then…

Sharon paused as she felt someone walk over her grave. She continued reading…

Four wives, all I loved, all I lost bar Pamela who I hope will not be charged and will live a happy life from my wealth. The other three, may they rest in hell with the men that took them from me. Of course, they were not the start of all of this, that priest…can you imagine being abused at a young age by someone who is supposed to be caring for you and preaching love?

Again, Sharon stopped and thought. *No! You don't justify all this for that.* She continued to read…

Anyway, I deserved better. Money does not make up for true love or real feeling. Many did not know that my injuries would finally kill me. I would have been lucky to make Christmas day.

Sharon pulled the second page of the letter to the front.

This is to put you out of your misery. Although shocking, there was a need for all the deaths.

Sharon stopped reading, stood and walked around the coffin a couple of times. Knowing she had to continue reading she kissed the coffin feeling the support of her missing friend beside her. Sat again, she continued to read.

The Twelve Days of Christmas

12 Drummers Drumming – Helmut Bopp my first Swiss banker who after some years, stole many millions from me.

11 Pipers Piping – Edinburgh, where I met and fell in love with my first wife Kate while at university. No target just memories smashed.

10 Lords a Leaping – Frank Kent, the Arts Minister who took Kate from me although they were never married. A renowned womanizer was Kent.

9 Ladies Dancing – the Ibiza club where I met Sharon Turner, my second wife. If you check she still part-owns the club that was bombed.

8 Maids a Milking – my true love, Vanessa Gresham, we never married but she was my secret mistress for many years…again until the crash.

7 Swans a Swimming - Hannah was Kent's stepdaughter with Vanessa Gresham. She was adopted, and no one…or few knew.

6 Geese a Laying – Haribe airport is where Sharon and I started our honeymoon.

5 Golden Rings – not only the place of my third marriage but the priest Father Candel listened to me. I thought he would blow the cover of…you know who. Unfortunately, Father Candel was a supporter of what was going on. The bastard married me there!

4 Calling Birds – the bastard, hidden by his position.

3 French Hens – all loved, all lost, all dead. My money was seeking loveless wives!

2 Turtle Doves - Dale Teldove and Roman Italo both took my women.

My Partridge in a Pear Tree – Pamela, I wish her a happy life in my previously favourite home—Pear Tree, Washington.

Many years of sitting in a wheelchair, thinking, gave me the idea. The song is virtually a perfect representation of my life, although stretched a little in part. I had the motive and the millions to pay any organization or person to carry out precisely what I wanted. Revenge is sweet!

Ho Ho Ho!

The End

Ken Kirkberry books:

Enlightenment young adult/coming of age Sci fi trilogy:

Enlightenment: This Earth

Enlightenment: Another Earth

Enlightenment: Colliding Earths

The Figure - a gripping crime story

The Equals – horror based crime story

Find out more:

https://www.amazon.co.uk/Ken-Kirkberry/e/B0722YXS97/ref=sr_ntt_srch_lnk_1?qid=1523824003&sr=8-1

https://www.facebook.com/ken.kirkberry.9

Printed in Great Britain
by Amazon